No Man's LAND

A Rebel Wayfarers MC & Incoherent MC
Crossover Story

MariaLisa deMora

Edited by Hot Tree Editing

Proofreading by Whiskey Jack Editing

Photography: CJC Photography

Model: Jamieson Fitzpatrick

Originally published in the charity anthology *Love, Loyalty and Mayhem MC*

First Published 2019

ISBN 13: 978-1-946738-50-9

DEDICATION

To those among us who recognize and seize opportunities,
you're blazing the way. Thank you.

Contents

ACKNOWLEDGMENTS

When I was approached about creating a brand new story as part of an anthology, the first thing that struck me was the name. *Love, Loyalty and Mayhem MC*. Those words helped lay the groundwork for the story you're about to read.

My main character personifies all aspects of that title in all the right ways. To him the brotherhood is everything he needed. Hitch is my badass hero who wakes up in hell, then thinks he's gone to heaven when he meets Talia. This story has caused the axis of my MC universe to tilt, bringing my RWMC and NTNT worlds into alignment in ways that should give you a glimpse of so much more to come. I hope you enjoy it.

The anthology went on to be wildly successful, making the *Wall Street Journal* and *USA TODAY* best-selling books list. In the process we also raised thousands of dollars for a charity called Bikers Against Bullies USA. I'm humbled and proud to have been part of the anthology team. A huge shout out to all twenty authors involved, because we really lived the motto: Teamwork makes the dream work. Special thank yous to Ryan Michele and Chelsea Camaron for blazing the trail.

So much love for the authors, readers, bloggers, reviewers, and everyone else who shared information about the anthology. Your support means so very much.

Woofully yours,

~ML

No Man's Land

Members of the Incoherent MC are no strangers to the pull and tug of disagreements with other clubs in their territory. But waking awash in the bloody aftermath of war's opening salvo wasn't typical.

After the slaughter of Hitch's brothers, he has two goals.

One, keep breathing long enough to avenge them.

Two, learn all there is to know about the angel who saved his life.

Talia had successfully wedged her way into the fringes of her brother Ewell's motorcycle club despite his attempts to keep her out. Her EMT skills come into play more often than she'd like, and when the IMC, a friendly rival club, asks the Jailbreakers MC for a favor, Ewell—and Talia—can't turn them down. Even if the aftermath means Talia could be drawn into the maelstrom of war between clubs.

Waking Up In Hell

I blinked up at a flat surface hovering overhead. It took a minute, but I decided it was a ceiling, dotted with tiny flecks of crimson. I watched in idle fascination as a fly crept closer and closer to one of the largest spots. Clearing my throat, I tried to swallow, not finding enough spit in my mouth. A painfully dry click echoed through my head, sounding frighteningly close to the slide of a gun cocking. I squinted as the fly broached the edge of that circle of red, no doubt drinking his buggy fill of my life's blood.

Another attempt to clear my throat was no more successful than the first, but the resulting pain in my middle was new. My eyes squeezed shut when I choked, having to brutally smother an urge to cough, already dreading whatever my next move needed to be.

My lungs ached with the longing to suck in a big ole breath, but every attempt fell short, slashed into shreds and leaving me panting. That pain slipped away, like the backwash of a wave, and I relaxed into the easy numbness it left behind, forgetting there was always another wave.

It came roaring back with a vengeance, tightening my muscles until I was sure my bones would break. Rolling over me, churning me into pieces, wedging itself between all the bits of me, the pain separated my mind from my body, and I groaned at the release. The echoing sound did more to map my surroundings than my eyes had done.

It was a large and open space. Flat out on the floor, I tried to lift my arm. Heavier than anything I expected, it twitched, a promising movement accompanied by an odd rustling. I tried again and managed to lift my hand from where it had been sprawled next to my body. My palm landed on my belly, and I had a frozen instant of terror when all I felt was fabric, but then I slid my fingers farther across and encountered that familiar stiff resistance that could only be leather.

No matter what else happened, this discovery left me giddy, because if I died right here and now, it'd be in my goddamned cut.

An attempt to lift my head sent me soaring, so dizzy and lightheaded I was floating without a tether. The clunk of my skull hitting the hard floor drove me back into myself, the pain taking up so much room it wasn't clear how I'd keep it company in my skin. The next try was more successful.

Eventually, I had my chin buried against my chest, gaze roaming what I could see of the room.

Alone.

Door open.

Everywhere I looked was draped in plastic, and on that plastic were drying splashes and sheets of red.

Something jutted from my side, and I spider-walked my hand across my body until I could grip whatever it was, wanting to fling it away. That proved impossible, and just the attempt woke the pain monster, so I struggled to simply pull it free. Extending my arm to its limit finally gained my objective, and I stared at the foot-long blade in disbelief before my hand spasmed and the dagger clattered to the floor.

Motors roaring outside abruptly expanded my awareness, and I listened intently, hearing the barest hint of voices over the rumbling of exhaust and engines. Gradually all sounds diminished, moving off into the distance in staggered groups of noise until silence reigned.

I looked at the ceiling, noticing the fly had been joined by dozens of its family and friends.

The muscles in my neck gave way in fits and jerks until my head rested on the cold plastic again.

My eyes closed, and in that comforting darkness, I finally found relief.

***

The buzzing was louder when I gained consciousness again. Hundreds of clusters of those damn flies were everywhere. Since I was still breathing and determined to vacate this hellhole, I wedged my elbows underneath me and pushed up, gravity nearly winning the battle when my head swung loosely on my neck, dipping backwards towards the floor for long enough to give me an upside-down view of something I hadn't expected and never wanted to see. Three bodies lay behind me, stacked neatly into a row next to the wall, each rolled in a shroud of clear plastic, faces distorted and gray.

Still I knew them.

My brothers.

Trammer, who'd grown up at my mom's table, seated side by side with me for most meals. His father was a waste of space, and his mother'd gotten hooked on dope our junior year.

Graceless, the man who'd taught me the full meaning of the saying that accidents wait for audiences. I'd helped him pick his bike up more than anyone else I knew.

Had known. *Fuck.*

Pizzaboy, who'd so wanted to be called Donatello—and us being the fucktards we were, we hadn't given him that moniker. Instead, we'd labeled him after his favorite food.

Such was the nature of our lives where names were given, not taken, and being a brother meant so much more than blood.

I flipped to the side, or attempted to, managing a slow roll. My blood-saturated clothing unstuck from the plastic with an obscene sucking sound. My side ached like a bitch, but the crippling pain seemed to have packed its bags and vamoosed. *Thank God*. If I could just get to my feet, I'd be set.

There was no noise other than the flies and crinkling of the plastic. No voices. No traffic near or in the distance. Just me, and three bodies wrapped for a delivery I was gonna do my damnedest to derail.

I surveyed the room, baffled why I wasn't in the same shape as them. This much blood meant I lay in what my brothers had spilled, along with what had seeped out of me from that pigsticker.

On hands and knees, I wobbled for a moment, swaying backwards and forwards like a windblown tube man in front of a pop-up pawn store. If anyone came through the door, any fighting I tried would be about as effective as those arm-waving freaks. Finally overbalancing in the direction where I aimed, I rocked back onto my heels, pushing upright. I looked down my torso at the blood and rips in my shirt and realized I'd be lucky if I found only the one hole in me.

With the hilt of the blade in my hand, I considered the length and heft of it, finally taking a moment to slide the tip between the leather of my belt and my jeans, seating the handle snug against my hip. As long as I didn't fall down and stab myself on it, it'd be good to have a weapon. I could already tell the holster at my back was empty, as was the one under my arm, and my boots were too light to still be hiding my knives. Running bare had never suited me, not since I found the truth behind club wars and desperate assholes unconcerned with family or innocent victims.

I studied the plastic-wrapped bodies, a chill pebbling my skin as I realized they'd been similarly stripped, but while I still wore my vest, theirs were gone.

Music played abruptly, as if it had woken up midsong and was determined to see the tune to its end. I jerked so hard I nearly fell over. It cycled through the few notes again, then fell silent. Somewhere close by was a phone, and if I could find it and it was one of ours, I could make a call that would start the wheels of rescue, recovery, and revenge. Club officers were keyed to all authorized devices, and with the tap of a finger, I'd reach salvation.

The phone helpfully played that damn song again; it was coming through the open door. I hadn't made it to my feet before the sound died away, and perched wavering on one knee, I could have screamed at the damned silence. Finally vertical, I staggered to the doorway and clung to the wood like a leech, trying to remain upright while the world swung in wide circuits.

The same do-do do-do-do-do music ricocheted through my head, and I zeroed in on the location before turning loose of the doorframe. A saddlebag lay on the floor, propped next to a battered dining room table in the center of the room. Black leather poked out of it. After a year of staggering through the open space between me and it, I stumbled to a stop next to the table. I kept my hand flat on the wooden surface in an attempt to stay upright, unsure I'd make it back on my feet if I went down again. Digging through the vests, I did my best to ignore the patches and names, titles and regions—each a memory shared with one of the bodies growing cold in the other room—until I found the device.

The music started again. The screen said *Kate Calling,* and my eyes closed. That was Trammer's ole lady. I declined the call, used my thumbprint to unlock the phone, and dialed from memory.

Until Rampage answered, I hadn't realized the pounding in my head was from holding my breath. "Tram," he said, his voice free and easy, ready to joke and shoot the shit with a brother. "What the fuck you need, man? I got a case'a suds and a screen, and there's a damn game on, which means I got my feet up while I swear at the TV."

"Ram." I startled, pain blooming in my side. I didn't recognize my own voice, rough and hoarse, like death had camped out in my throat. "Ram."

"The fuck?" Background sound on his end of the call muted, and he asked, "Tram? What's up, brother?" I didn't answer him. Couldn't while the eagerness—the raw need in his voice to help, however it was needed, throttled my words. "Trammer, where the fuck are you, man?"

"Tram—" I swallowed and tried again. "Trammer's dead. Graceless and Pizzaboy, too. Ram, I been stabbed. I don't—" The room swung in a slow circle, and when I closed my eyes, it sped up, with me as a focal point while it whirled. "I'm not—"

"Where?" He was begging, and I knew all I had to do was give him a direction, tell him a location, suss out an address, and he'd be here. No questions asked. That's what true brothers did. When I stayed silent, he tried again. "What's happened?" I struggled to answer, my mouth dry as dust, tongue stuck to the back of my teeth. "Who's this? Who's got Tram's phone?"

"Hitch." I finally named myself, and that settled me in a weird way. If I could say my own name, if I could speak that truth, I could do the rest that he needed. "Hitch. Ram, we're... I don't know. It's a house or something. In the—" I was about to say woods, but I didn't know anything other than the room where I'd woken and this table. I stared at the windows across the front of the building, seeing green globes of trees, but not woods. "In a grove. I can't hear anything."

"Where's Tram?"

I wished my voice would fail again. Wished my words would dry up and drift away, because to speak it aloud would make it true. "Dead."

"Fuck."

Even if he couldn't see me, I nodded in agreement, gagging when the movement set the room to swaying again.

"Look at the map on Tram's phone, see if you can figure out where you are." The sound quality had grown an echo. "You're on speaker, my old lady's walking out now. You can say what you need. I'm gonna rally the boys, and we'll come, Hitch. Swear on my grave, we'll come."

With that inauspicious phrasing ringing in my ears, I fumbled the device, fingers determined to send it plunging to the hard floor until I wrestled them into submission, dropping it only an inch onto the table. The clatter must have been louder to Rampage, and he yelled, "What's happening?"

"Nothing," I tried to say, but the absurdity rolled over me, and I chunked out a laugh, carving it into pieces until it fell apart on the air. "Dropped the phone. I'm—" I poked the screen with a fingertip, putting Rampage on speaker and then opening the correct app on only the second try. A big green dot pulsed in the center of a swath of darker green, and I maneuvered the map until it pulled back, showing more green, finally broken on the north edge by a red line. "Highway…uh. State highway. A road. Meridian.

I'm—" I made the map slide from side to side until I found a wide blue line. "I'm west of the interstate, just south of Meridian." Frustrated, I poked around until the map finally gave up the most useful information. "I'm here. We're here at Stone McCauley Groves." The place was smack in the middle of unclaimed territory, and we'd always called it "No Man's Land."

"On our way." Rampage must have realized how reluctant I was to sever this lifeline. "I got the boys, and we're comin', Hitch. We're comin'."

"Hurry." Voice roughened with anger and pain, I tried to urge him, only I was speaking to dead air.

***

I'd first become aware of the Incoherent Motorcycle Club when Trammer and I were in high school. We'd been hanging around the local drive-in, ogling the flirty waitresses flitting around on roller skates, when the ground under our feet literally began to shake. Within moments, it was as if a mob of motorcycles had swarmed the parking lot, unmitigated chaos to my eyes. The men had parked their bikes, dismounted, and slung arms around the women who'd ridden in with them. While my mind had insisted there'd been hundreds of bikes, only ten men sauntered underneath the overhang and claimed two of the picnic tables.

Trammer, named after a suburb in faraway Michigan where he'd lived as a child, leaned across our table, only three down from the black-leather-clad bikers, and hissed excitedly. "Did you see?" He rolled his eyes towards the bikers, then back to me. "So cool, man."

I lifted my chin and grunted, my disinterest entirely affected. Someone sat heavily beside me, and I turned to see Karen crowding close, her long legs folded awkwardly underneath the table. A girl who I sometimes dated, she rolled the wheels on her skates back and forth, and nervously laughed.

"Mikey, would you take their order for me?"

Michael Hitchcock was me, Mike to my friends, Mikey to Karen and only allowed because I'd boned her. I'd not yet earned Hitch as a nickname but had tried it out on mirror-me once or twice. I liked it so far.

"Mr. Thomas said I've got to wait on them 'cause it was my turn when they came in."

"Why don't you?" Trammer curled his lip at Karen. "Too good for 'em?"

"No." She huffed. "I just... They scare me, okay?"

I cut a glance over to the tables and caught the eye of one of the men. He nodded at me, and smiled, then turned back to give the woman perched on his knee a different kind of smile.

"Sure, I'll do it." I pushed up from the table and snagged her ticket book. "You sit here and try not to kill anybody."

Trammer and Karen weren't each other's biggest fans, Trammer certain she was trying to get between us and being all "bros before hos" about it. Karen said Trammer wanted in her pants, which was certainly true. He'd fuck anything standing still. "Be right back."

As I neared the tables, I became acutely aware of the differences between me—high school cool in my half-laced sneaks and tight, ripped jeans, a faded graphic-tee sagging around my too-thin shoulders—and the men seated on the table and benches. Each wore what was undoubtedly a uniform of sorts. They were dressed in dark jeans made of thick fabric for hard use, scuffed black leather boots, shirts of varying colors, most with a distinctive shield proclaiming their devotion to a brand of motorcycle, and a black leather vest. Whether snapped in the front, held together with swinging chains, or draping along their sides, each proudly bore a fabric patch in the center of their back.

"Hey," I offered, coming to a stop about three feet away. "Do you know what you want?"

One man at the far table—the only one without a woman on his knee—scoffed far back in his throat. "Wanted that pretty chickie to come be my sidepiece for the day." The men around him laughed, women ducking their chins and tittering. Others took up the idea, and I heard other, more indecent suggestions about how Karen could service them.

The third time I heard, "She could suck my cock, too," Karen's ticket book crumpled in my fist.

The man seated nearest where I stood never took his eyes off me as he barked out, "Shut it." I tried to hold his gaze, but the weight of it was massive, as if there was a repellant force causing my eyes to dip. "Boy, she means something to you, ain't no shame in steppin' up and dealin' with assholes disrespecting your girl." The other men had stopped talking when he ordered them, and silence was thick around the tables now. "She don't, and you're just painfully unaware of the ways of men and women, that's a different kind of lesson I ain't up for teachin' today."

I cut my eyes up and found his face. Not smiling, not scowling, he looked open and somehow confused.

"She's my girlfriend." I shrugged. "I'm here because you scared her, without her even talking to you. Now..." I tried to mimic the scoff the other man made, the sound coming out weak and frightened. I winced. "Now I understand why."

"She suck your cock?" The original speaker opened his mouth wide, waggling his tongue obscenely. "I could teach her if she don't."

The leader—I took him to be that with how they'd quieted a moment ago—looked at me with a "what now" expression. Tearing my gaze from him, I fixed the other one with a stare I hoped could pierce through his ignorance, and told him clearly, "Shut up. What happens between me and her isn't your business. Now, do you want food or not?"

"Oh, boy's got some nads, Twisted." The instigator hadn't taken offense at my declaration and seemed somehow pleased. "Might wanna get his name, see if he grows into 'em over the next couple of years."

Twisted, evidently the leader, grinned broadly. "Might do that, Catfish. Might do." He angled his body and looked at the men around him, getting a nod from each before he turned back to face me. "What's your name, boy?"

I stared at him, my brain considering and discarding all options before I told him the truth. "I'm Hitch."

That had been ten years ago. I'd been a member of the Incoherent MC for eight, an officer for four.

***

Engines and voices startled me awake, and I grunted as my back arched against the hard surface I was lying on. I was immediately convinced that whoever had started this tango was back to end the dance. I'd pulled the sticker from my belt when I'd assumed this position on the table, and the handle was clasped in my grip as I fought through the pain to sit.

Facing the door, I stayed where I was, mostly because I wasn't certain my legs would bear my weight. Those half breaths had my ribs gnawing at my sides, begging to be stretched and strained, promising to make me buckle with pain. Woozy, I pulled my hand from around my middle where it was holding me together and thudded it against the table to keep from falling on my face.

Words and sounds buzzed as unintelligibly as the flies until I heard one voice clearly and knew who spoke.

"If Hitch said Trammer was dead, same for Graceless and Pizzaboy, and he's alive to make a call, I'm not standing around here with my thumb up my ass while you decide what you want to do." Catfish was our VP, and even after everything that had gone down the first time I met him, had been my sponsor to get my chance to prospect for the club. I trusted him as much as I did Trammer, which meant with my life.

"Here." The intended shout was weaker than I expected, so I pulled in another half breath that burned all the way down and pushed it back out on a yell. "I'm here."

Bootheels thudded against packed dirt, then cement, and then they were bursting through the door. Rampage came straight to me. Hands on my shoulders, he swept me up and down, then spoke over his shoulder, "Wave Dyno in, then call and tell him no need to dispatch the second van." He shook his head when he looked at me, brows pulling down in a dark scowl. "He's ambulatory, at least."

"You gonna poke me with that, brother?" When Catfish took the blade, I realized I'd been pointing it towards the door, and unintentionally directly at him. "Lemme have it a minute, yeah? I'll just hold it for ya."

"No, man. They left that in me." I tried for humor as I gestured towards my side, even knowing it'd fall flat. "I'm attached to it now."

Catfish plucked my shirt free from where it'd dried stuck to my skin, and I heard a rip followed by cool air that raised the hair on my arms. "Fuck, man. There's definitely a hole ain't supposed to be there."

My chuckle turned into a cough that threatened to rip my guts out.

Rampage asked, "Anything else, Hitch?"

I shook my head, more an "I don't know" than a "nope," and he understood, giving me a quick going-over. His fingers discovered two tender places on my head, one with a knot big enough to make him *tsk* far back in his throat. Another hole in one arm, something he deemed a through-and-through shot, so I guessed at least a fair amount of the blood I wore was my own.

The other men had fanned out through the structure, and I knew when they found the abattoir, the shouts and curses louder before dying off as the gravity of what had happened here struck each of my brothers.

"Where's Rags?" My words came out in fits and starts, syllables strung together by threads of pain as Rampage and Catfish braced me, my arms over their shoulders. They lifted and let me find my balance, feet flat on the floor instead of toes dragging behind. *I'll thank them later.*

Rags, or Ragman, was our president, a leader like no other. A man who'd been through enough shitty times between drug cartel invasions and club wars to know how best to avoid them in today's club climate. Until he wasn't present, I didn't know how much I'd hoped to see him. If Ragman was here—or Twisted, our national president, and the first man in my life to tell it like it was—I'd know in my bloody gut everything'd be okay.

"Workin' the horn." Catfish dipped to the side, and when he came back up, I saw he'd grabbed the bag with our brothers' vests. "We got nothin' in the air on this shit goin' down, and once we had a lock on your location, Dyno activated the drones and saw the locale, including the lack of company." He angled his neck, face turned to me. "Thought we'd have to handcuff Rags or some shit. Finally convinced him to call national." That was his way of tellin' me Ragman's absence wasn't anything to do with me. "Three of our own dead, our enforcer bleedin' out—he's got to sort this shit now."

Multiple exhausts sounded in the distance, and I swallowed. If my brothers were in here with me, there was only one truth of who could be headed in. "Think you can give me back the sticker? Or better yet, dig through there"—I dipped my head toward the bag in Catfish's hand—"and find my iron?"

Strangely calm, he tightened his arm around my shoulders and steadied me against his side. "Nah, brother," he said with a twist of his lips. "Listen."

I did.

Ride of the Valkyries.

"Fuck me."

He nodded. "Dyno. We made him stay back at the highway with half the men. He's got the eyes in the sky on his phone, so we waved him in a few minutes ago."

Dyno was our tech guru, and he had a thing for some Coppola war movie made in the previous century. The flick had featured Wagner's epic song in a crucial scene, and he was prone to blasting it when we rode to war.

Within a minute, the room was filled with a wall of flesh willing to stand between me and whatever might come. Men who followed the code of brotherhood, believing a man was only as good as his word and wrongs were best righted with might. My brothers, members of the Big Bend chapter of the Incoherent MC. Our clubhouse was outside Tallahassee, and our territory stretched for miles along the Gulf Coast. Men I trusted, could count on, and all of which were, at this moment, pissed as fuck about what had happened to me, Trammer, Graceless, and Pizzaboy.

***

Dyno came directly to me, brows drawn into a deep frown. He held a tablet aimed in my direction and spoke to the air, either recording or streaming. "Fucking hell, Hitch might be on his feet, but our boy ain't lookin' good."

I closed my eyes when I heard the voices of two men who weren't present, telling me Dyno was facilitating a video conference with the leaders of our club.

Ragman's hissed "Jesus" was overridden by Twisted's demand, "Tell me what the fuck went down, Hitch."

Since I'd woken the first time, coming to surrounded by blood and death, I'd been piecing everything together, knowing the first chance I had to tell it would need to be accurate and as articulate as possible.

"We were at Hot Lips."

A bar owned by the wife of a retired biker from the frozen north, Hot Lips was the local hangout for our club. Houlihan was her official name, but her old man, Hawk, still called her Hot Lips often. He'd been president of the North Chicago chapter of the Rebel Wayfarers MC, moving to Florida when it was time to fly the icy coop. He wore support patches for the RWMC, us, and the Jailbreakers. No conflict there, since our clubs were tightly twined together these days with both blood ties and patchovers.

"Graceless got a call someone broke into his ole lady's car."

We'd been seated at a booth, discussing an upcoming poker run, when his phone rang. I'd heard every shrill word and had winced on his behalf at how scared she'd sounded. I'd exchanged a glance with Trammer, dug out my wallet, and dropped bills on the table, ready to roll at my brother's back in an instant. That's just what we did.

"She works at that place out on Pommel, the booze warehouse."

We'd rolled up loud and proud, no hiding who we were or why we were there. Our bikes had surrounded her car, which had been pushed up close to the back of the building.

It had been turned sideways between two columns and wasn't just broken into—it had been trashed, windows shattered and hood caved in.

"We thought we heard her call out from inside the loading docks."

We'd dismounted, listening to Graceless cussing and shouting at the cost, the waste, the ignorance of it all. The pain in her voice had taken us off guard, and the three of them had rushed inside without utilizing any caution, no matter how I shouted. My role in the club meant I knew better, and my inability to control my brothers had led directly to their deaths.

Dyno stared at me over the tablet, understanding dawning in his expression.

"It happened fast. I didn't really see anything. Darkness and blurs. When I came to, I was here. From there to then, nothin'." I stiffened my spine, pushing upright and taking my weight off Catfish's and Rampage's shoulders. I wished I could see Twisted and Ragman's faces, wished I could know if they blamed me like I did myself. Wished for clear knowledge of what had happened. "I take responsibility." A jerk of my head woke the pain in my middle, and it coiled like a snake about to strike. "It's on me."

"Unless you held the blade and gun, our brothers' deaths ain't on you. Ambush like that? Wouldn't have mattered what you said or did once you were in their noose. Do not take that shit on, brother." Twisted's voice was flat, filled with certainty, and told me he'd brook no argument. "I got a lead on some shit. Ragman, I'ma be rollin' that way in five. Catfish, you and Ram get Hitch to the Jailbreakers house in Adkins, man. They're gonna help get him patched up. If at all possible, I want him ready to rock and roll when Rags and I get there, you get me?" Ram grunted his agreement. His outline was wavering, the edges of his face blurring.

Twisted's voice echoed through the room, a surreal soundtrack to my loss. "We got you, brother. Be there soon."

After a final look at the room where I should have died, I turned my back on the shack and leaned heavily on my brothers as we walked into the hot Florida sunshine.

The van ride lasted for at least a hundred excruciating days. Not only was the suspension way past needing work, and jounced around at the least provocation, but the cargo laid out in front of me meant I spent the time in dark contemplation. Side by side, shoulder to shoulder, my brothers were stretched across the width of the vehicle, heels towards the back doors. We'd left them in the plastic shrouds, figuring it was the cleanest way to transport them.

We weren't preserving evidence for the officials. No need. I didn't worry about how the details would be sorted out; we had enough cops in our pocket that it'd happen however Twisted and Rags wanted it.

What we were damned sure doing was preserving their dignity, same as we'd do for any fallen brother.

I couldn't tear my gaze away from Trammer. I tortured myself imagining his last minutes. Picturing what my mother's face would look like when I told her he was dead. He had a woman and a little girl, and their coming life's weight of grief bore down on me.

Pickle, one of the men who'd ridden in the van, spoke from over my head, "We'll get 'em."

"Yeah," I gritted out, fingers sliding as I pressed against the bleeding wound in my side. "Yeah, we will."

IMC was a club used to violence. We didn't deal it in regularly, but we wouldn't shy away when necessary. From the looks on my brothers' faces back at the grove shack, I wouldn't be running alone when I tracked down the bastards who'd spilled my blood and taken the breath from our brothers.

The next bouncing jar nearly shattered my control. The pain was like a fishhook lodged deep inside my chest, anchored in the bedrock of agony and rage. I'd already decided I'd try to not let them sideline me, no matter the consensus on my injuries. Rampage had bandaged my arm before I'd loaded myself into the van, but I hadn't let him take my cut off to do more. Call me superstitious, but it seemed like retaining it and the breath in my body had to be connected. In my own mind, I'd vowed to not remove it until everything was done and whoever had killed my brothers shared their fate.

As the van slowed, Dyno called out from behind the wheel, "Bump, brother." I gritted my teeth through the series of suspension-yawing potholes with only a muffled grunt. "Sorry, man," Dyno muttered as Pickle's hand landed on my shoulder. His fingers wrapped in the leather and helped keep me upright as the van lurched around a final corner and rocked to a stop.

The back doors opened, and Rampage stood there with Catfish, lines of grief etching their features. Unfamiliar faces crowded behind them, men's gazes cataloging the contents of the van with muttered curses. One man pushed up beside Catfish. Gaze fixed on the bodies, he thrust out his hand towards Catfish and offered us welcome. "Be welcome, IMC. Ain't gonna lie and say it's good to see you guys. Sucks the reason." His nameplate declared him Sparks, and under that, an officer's plate titled him President, obviously of the Jailbreakers. I hadn't much contact with them officially, just a few members here and there. Seemed like good men. They were all about the brotherhood and making life better for their members. From what I heard, they followed protocol, and that went a long way to keeping a club from straying too far from its stated mission or motto.

Catfish took his wrist and gripped, their shake going up and down twice before releasing. "Appreciated, man."

"Twisted done called and gave me the rundown. We got a couple of rooms set up with what we thought you'd need." He lifted his chin to me, and I returned the gesture. "If you wanna climb out that side door, we got an EMT ready for you. You're Hitch, right?" I dipped my head in a brief nod. "Yeah, let's get you situated. Then we'll give honor to your men."

The door beside me opened, and Rampage was there. Determined to not show weakness in front of strangers, I took a moment to convince my body to move, and after I slung my legs over the edge, it was an easy transition to standing. Not so easy to keep that position, but thankfully Ram was there to keep me from taking a header. *Fuck*. A swath of blood smeared from where I'd been propped against the back of the front seat to the door—could have only come from me.

"Ram," I said on a grunt. I waited for his muttered response and acknowledged, "I might need some help."

"No shit, Sherlock." His arm slipped under mine, shoulder wedging me upright.

Pickle was on the other side, and it took everything in me to manage it, but I put one foot in front of the other until we got to the back of the van. They paused when I did, and I turned my head to stare at Sparks.

"All respect." That was as close to thanks as I would get when talking to an officer of another club, not wanting any chance of obligating my brothers for anything.

He lifted his chin again and responded, "No worries."

The pain was so bad my head hung low by the time Ram and Pickle got me to the door of the Jailbreakers clubhouse, a single-story ranch-style building that had been added to on both sides, creating wide wings. There were dozens of bikes in the front lot, and from the cooling ticks coming from the engines, I deduced most were ours, which meant Jailbreakers probably had a parking lot out back for their own bikes.

Together, Ram and Pickle lifted me over the threshold and into cool dimness. Walls had been taken out in places, making the space stretch across a good length of the building. It was furnished with couches and chairs, a small bar in one corner, and three TVs mounted to the walls. It was also filled with men and women and children, which told me the Jailbreakers had gone on lockdown, and the fact they still took us in meant a lot. We'd probably be stretching their hospitality thin.

If the Jailbreakers were on lockdown with families in play, that meant— "Graceless. His ole lady? Is Dottie—"

Pickle's head went side to side, and Rampage made a pained sound. "Fuck."

I'd sat at their table for many a meal, her softly scolding Roger, Graceless' government name, about his manners. Dottie was a sweet woman who worked hard and loved the club nearly as much as her ole man had.

"Where'd they leave her?" I hadn't seen her at the shack. Only two rooms and both mapped easily even in my state. No way I would have missed seeing her if she were there.

"Tow driver called it in about thirty minutes ago. He was picking up an abandoned car and found her in the back seat. No doubt they did her after they got what they really wanted." I couldn't tear my gaze away from Pickle's clear pain. "From what was said, it was quick at least."

Sometimes a body had to take comfort in the small things.

Rampage asked the room, "Know where the EMT's at?"

Two men pointed towards a hallway, and one said, "Second door on the left."

That short pause had settled into my bones, and it turned out starting walking a second time was so much harder than the first. My heavy head dragged at my neck, and I watched my boots stumbling and twisting underneath me until I was walking on air, leather of my soles never striking the floor as my brothers took my weight, lifting me up.

The room swirled, corners coming close and receding in turn until I was disoriented. A high bed stood central to the space, and along the walls were cabinets with sinks and drawers. It looked like a clinic, and that struck me funny.

I heard Pickle's muttered question, "What's he laughing at?"

"No idea. He's been in and out of it since we got there." Ears buzzing, I nearly missed his next words as the bed came up to meet my back. "It's a goddamned miracle he made it."

My gaze stuck on a dark spot on the faraway ceiling, a fleck, a speck, a tiny dot of something that grew until it swallowed me whole.

Into the Darkness

Talia

When Talia's brother had first called, she'd been annoyed at being woken in the middle of the afternoon. Working third shift on the ambulance meant her days only held the most restless of slumber, and she had been chasing a sweet dream before the jangle of his ringtone dragged her back to consciousness. They had a texting relationship, and she knew he wouldn't dial unless it was dire, so she'd shoved that irritation down and answered.

Three minutes later, she'd dashed water in her face and shoved her feet into utility boots on her way out the door.

Ewell had launched his MC years ago, needing to surround himself with strong men with morals. Their neighborhood growing up hadn't been the best, and he'd wandered down a bleak path for a very long time, finally dragging his life out of the darkness by strength of will. The club provided the framework to be the man he should have always been, and he saw it as a chance to give others the same opportunity.

They were the Jailbreakers, and their name didn't refer to any bent towards busting brothers out of jail but focused on tearing down the prisons men made for themselves. The learned behaviors that conspired to send them behind bars again and again. If Ewell, known as Sparks to his men, could put a stop to the cycle, he could keep more men free—like him.

As a male-dominated club, they'd had their fair share of altercations. When she'd gained enough knowledge from her studies to be useful, Ewell started calling her for help as needed. For a long time, she had gotten more practice stitching up his men than the pig feet the medical school issued. She gained her EMT license, ready to work the rest of her way through school. With the club's frequent need for assistance, she'd been doubly glad for the breadth of knowledge since.

As the club had grown, so had the scope of the altercations, until they no longer had one-on-one fights but club versus club. Ewell and his men knew outing her as their medical professional would scrap her license and ruin her professional plans, so they were careful to keep Talia hidden from all but the most trusted of their friends. Seeing how Ewell had developed into a mentor for his men, maturing in ways she hadn't thought possible, she'd do anything for the club.

After arriving at the clubhouse today, she'd laid out supplies based on threadbare information. Male victim—*duh, it's always the men*—gunshot and stabbed. Talia'd been making coffee when the unmistakable sound of women and children trickled in from the front rooms. Having family at the compound wasn't unheard of since the Jailbreakers were family oriented, but with her being called in too, this was unusual enough to note.

When a mass of motorcycles had roared up, she'd watched through the window as a van had driven into view and immediately been surrounded by Ewell and his men. More men in black leather vests crowded around, all bearing the patch of the Incoherent MC, another club with roots in the area. *What in the world?* The back doors opened, and she'd gasped. There were six boots in view, three pair, toes up, all unmoving.

Ewell greeted one of the men, and there was a muted mumble through the glass of the window as they briefly discussed something; then the van shifted and moved. A moment later, three men came around the side. The two on either side of the one who was clearly her patient held him upright, and he seemed barely conscious until he stopped next to Ewell. His head lifted and he said something.

He was gorgeous. Dark brown hair hung down either side of his face, and the apparent pain he was in made his brows gather together. With widely spaced dark eyes framed by cut cheekbones, and the added enhancement of a trimmed beard a shade darker than his hair, this man was everything any woman could want. His surge of energy faded as the moment ended, and his helpers started towards the front of the house.

When she rounded the corner to the hallway by the treatment room, she pushed past the men crowded around the door to the place she thought of as hers, shoving between them without apology. They were between her and the patient, and all she could think of was what she'd already heard and seen.

Women and children in the clubhouse unexpectedly.

Three dead men.

For some unknown reason, a friendly but rival club had brought those men here to her brother.

One of theirs was walking wounded, a man who, despite his clear pain and exhaustion, paused to pay respects to Ewell.

It all added up to something very bad going down, and she and her brother's club were right in the middle of it.

***

Talia

Inside the treatment room, the men positioned the injured man on the table as she pulled on gloves. *My patient*. He was out, which she decided to count as a boon. From the amount of blood soaking his clothing, she wanted him as calm and peaceful as possible.

"What happened?" Prepared for the need to cut his clothes off for treatment, Talia approached the table with scissors in hand and was surprised to find them plucked from her grip. Whirling to glare at the man who held them overhead, she snapped, "What the hell do you think you're doing?"

"His cut stays on." He gave her nothing more than that, and she let her gaze drop to the man's nameplate.

"Pickle?" He nodded. Without looking, she pointed at the man on the table behind her. "You want me to help him?" Pickle's mouth pulled to the side, but he nodded. "Then you got to trust me."

"His cut stays on." Now the other man in the room chimed in, and she tossed a dark glare his direction. "Sister."

Breaking the stare, she lifted a hand and tried to hide her surprise, thumbnail scratching her eyebrow. She knew from Ewell what this man had just called her was as much an honorific as ma'am. Pulling in a deep breath, she rolled her lips and shook her head, huffing air out her nose.

"You're already on my last nerve." There was a chuckle from the doorway, where Ewell parted the crowd and walked in. Ignoring the men who were frustrating her, she barked out, "They won't let me treat him. Why did you call me here if I'm not going to be allowed to do my job?"

"Sparks." Pickle addressed her brother, and she knew she'd lost any ground she might have gained. *Men.* "His cut stays on."

"Then his cut stays on." Ewell slipped an arm around Talia's waist and tugged her sideways for a hug. "But you get the fuck out of my sister's way and let her do her goddamned job."

Pickle shoved the scissors her direction, and she yanked them from his hand with her own version of a biker's scowl. Turning back to the table, Talia was once again struck by how handsome the man lying there was. But he was also pale, tinged with gray, and she knew she had to get to work.

One arm of his shirt had been ripped wide, with a makeshift bandage placed around the bicep. The hidden wound seemed to be the source of much of the blood soaking his clothing. Upon closer visual inspection, she saw a smaller tear in the fabric along his side, also surrounded by a decent amount of blood.

The second IMC member crowded close, and Talia flicked her hair back with a huff, glaring at him. This man, Rampage by his nameplate, gave her a concise rundown she didn't expect, ratcheting up her opinion of him by about a dozen notches.

"Upper arm is a GSW, through and through. He's got a stab wound in the abdominal upper-left quadrant by what appeared to be a ten-inch double-edged blade, removed before we arrived on scene. He's presenting with tenderness on that side, but there's also significant contusions indicative of blunt force trauma. Closed head injury with one distinct subdural hematoma and a secondary smaller one, both without palpable skull fractures. Respiration, pulse, both within normal range. Nominal confusion, but he's been in and out. Pupils normal and reactive, when he's got his peepers open." Rampage paused a beat then said, "If you'll pass me the scissors, I'll get his shirt off under his cut so you can look at his side."

Wordlessly, Talia handed them over, then ignored him working on the other side of the patient while she untangled the knots holding the strips of fabric in place on his arm. They worked together like that as she cleaned the hole bored through the flesh of the patient's arm before using tidy stitches to close the wound.

She had just finished bandaging the arm, about ready to move to the stab wound, when the man groaned and his eyes flickered, lashes fluttering against his cheeks. She bent over him with her hand on his other shoulder, prepared to hold him in place if he woke up combative. His eyes opened halfway, sleepy and unfocused, and so dark blue it was as if a piece of the evening sky had fallen there. Up this close, the dark hair at his temples was springy, curling in Florida's ever-present humidity. His gaze latched onto her, and Talia forgot to breathe. Even in this state, his stare was powerful. One corner of his mouth curved up, and he blinked languidly, as if nothing was going on, as if he hadn't been beaten, shot, and stabbed and wasn't still bleeding on her table.

"An angel," he murmured, and a weight landed on the back of her neck. His hand curved around and pulled down, down, down, until her lips brushed his. Gentle and soft, more a yearning caress than a kiss—still the electricity that sizzled through her was raw and powerful. Then he relaxed, losing consciousness again, eyes drifting closed as his hand fell away.

"God damn you, Hitch," Rampage muttered as she straightened. Talia turned to look at him, startled. He offered a wink, mouth twisted in a fake pout. "Even half dead as he is, he finds the prettiest woman in the room to hit on."

She rolled her eyes. "Whatever." *Men*.

He ducked his head, and she turned back to Hitch—her patient.

***

Hitch

Voices faded in and out. Whispers and murmurs, rough rumbling conversations that hovered on the edges of my mind. I was dreaming, but it felt so real, and I knew in my gut I was safe.

"Without imaging, I can't know for sure what kind of internal damage has been done." The woman's words were stark and spare, no discernable accent, but that was the norm for this stretch of Florida with such an influx of people from all over. Finding a true Floridian was rare.

There was the tiniest catch in her voice when she said, "The trajectory means it's likely low enough to have missed his kidney, spleen, pancreas, and stomach, but unless you let me take him to the hospital, we can't rule out bowel involvement."

Uh, nope. Not happening. They couldn't take me to a hospital, not without causing a whole lot of trouble. Even if I went on my own, given who I was and the club I claimed as my home, there'd be questions, an investigation, and the last thing any man like me wanted to do was invite the po-po all up in our shit.

My eyes wouldn't behave, staying stubbornly closed against all my attempts to pry them open. Same with my lips, those damned traitorous bastards.

A touch against the side of my face jolted me, the cool glide of a hand up and over my brow, then down along my cheek. The contact felt so good I wanted to lean into it, make it stay. There was a dusting of a caress across my lips that stroked my memory.

There'd been a woman. So goddamned beautiful, leaning over me. Dark hair twisted into a ponytail over one shoulder, she'd stared into me with her gorgeous brown eyes, sinking so deep I knew she'd seen the dark stains on my soul.

I'd kissed her. Kissed her and felt a connection that yet pulled at a space in my chest I'd thought forever empty.

The sounds became a mumbled buzz before thinning out to nothing.

My last memory was something I held tight to as I slid back into the darkness.

She'd kissed me back.

She's an Angel
Talia

She stared at Ewell, worrying the edge of her lip with her teeth. He knew enough to give her a little space so she could think through his request to stay at the clubhouse for the foreseeable future. He'd backed off a couple of steps to have a quiet conversation with two more IMC patch wearers who'd shown up not long ago. One was nondescript, a man who looked like he'd had a hard life but wasn't bitter about it. The other practically oozed danger. It flashed from his eyes when he'd stalked in, owning the room, no matter it belonged to her brother and his club. Bearded, long dark hair tied back into a thick braid, and even clubbed at the end it hung to the middle of his back.

She angled her gaze to where Hit—her *patient* was resting. It had become harder to keep a distance since he'd kissed her, but Talia was determined to be as professional as possible. He grimaced, muttering something unintelligible, and she pressed a hand to his forehead again. Still cool, thank God. Not only had Rampage opposed calling an ambulance—*oh, the irony, since we're both EMTs*—but so had her brother.

"Talia?" Ewell called her name, and three pairs of eyes locked on her. "We need someone to look at the bodies." He glanced at the two men, then back to her. "Please. Twisted"—he gestured towards the dark-haired man, and she stiffened. That name was one everyone who lived on the coast recognized. "He has a guy, but he can't be here for a few hours."

"Yeah." She sighed and was pulling away from the table when a hand grabbed her wrist. With a gasp, she looked down to see Hitch was awake and staring straight at her. It had been hours since she'd finished patching him up, and this was the first attentiveness he'd shown. "Hey—"

He cut her off with a brief shake of his head. His lips moved, but there was no sound.

"What?"

He mouthed something again, and she bent closer only to find she'd been duped when his other hand wrapped around the back of her neck, tugging her down. Bristly cheek pressed to hers, his mouth was beside her ear as he whispered, "Be careful, angel." There was a gentle glide against her cheek that could only be his lips as she pulled away. This time, instead of lapsing directly into unconsciousness, he stared right at her as he struggled to get an arm underneath him. Rampage helped pull him upright, taking the strain off Hitch's arm.

"Twisted." Hitch's voice was clear if raspy, and his gaze left her to go to where Ewell stood with Twisted and the other biker. "Ragman." He swallowed hard and winced. "What do we know?"

"Not here, brother." Hair raised all along her arms. Twisted's intonation was smooth and dark, the sound a deadly ocean undertow would make if given voice. "Not with citizens."

She shook her head. "Sparks." His nose wrinkled when she called his club name, knowing how she disliked using it. With her brother, with their family, there was a story behind everything, and this one could have ended in a different, deadly way. "Where are they?" She couldn't bring herself to say anything else.

Hitch's grip on her wrist tightened, and she flinched, surprised he held her with such strength. His voice was a harsh growl when he said, "I'll go with you." She turned to argue, but he was still staring across the room. "Brothers." Disappointment crossed his face, and he dipped his chin. "Much as I want to be in whatever comes next, I'm a liability right now and know it. Don't delay on me to do what you need to do."

"So noted, my brother. But we got a bit of waitin' to do," Twisted said. "Mayhap you will, mayhap you won't. We'll see when it's time."

"Talia." Ewell's tone was cautioning, but when Hitch pulled on her arm, she didn't resist, stepping closer to where he sat.

Something about the man was intriguing, beyond his looks and that surprising warning. The hours spent at his bedside hadn't been enough. She needed to know more about him. *Moth to a flame.*

"I'm good, Sparks." She let the half smile she'd given her brother slip from her lips before looking at Hitch. "Can you even stand? I'm not going to carry you." She knew her opinion was no threat for whatever he wanted to do and was unsurprised when he didn't answer.

Instead, he flashed her a smile and restated more firmly, "I'm going with you."

She fixed him with the sternest look she could muster. "If you rip my stitches out, I'll be testy."

Her scold earned another grin. Hitch's lips pulled sideways like he wanted to say something but was holding back. *Whatever.*

Her brother would have insisted on the same if it were his friends lying dead. *No use arguing with him.*

The bruising on Hitch's torso was extensive, but he didn't give any indication of pain when he shifted to dangle his legs over the side of the table. Rampage came to his side as Hitch's feet slipped to the floor. He wavered, gripped Ram's shoulder, and grunted once he looked like he was steady on his feet.

Talia found a strange expression of resignation on Ewell's face. She studied him, trying unsuccessfully to determine what it meant.

"Ready." Hitch curled his arm around hers, sandwiching Talia's elbow against his side as they passed the trio standing by the door. Twisted stared at her with a puzzled look, broken when he caught her gaze on him. A brilliant smile split his thick beard. So at odds to the anger and rage still in his eyes, it made Talia press closer to Hitch.

In the hallway, Ram led them deeper into the warren that made up the Jailbreakers clubhouse. Talia had been here often enough to know her way around. She knew where family and non-members were allowed and the places off-limits to anyone but officers. The direction they were headed was one of the latter, and she hemmed and hawed internally before quietly asking, "Are you sure this is where…"

Ram nodded. "Yeah, our men are back here. Earlier, Sparks told me how to find them."

Well then.

"What's your name, angel?" That was Hitch, and Talia found his gaze fixed on her, not where they were walking. "Sparks, the president here, he called you Talia? Is that your name?" She nodded. Something flashed in his eyes, and his jaw tightened as if with pain before he asked, "What's he to you?"

"Are you hurting? This was a bad idea." She tried to stop him, but the stubborn man wouldn't be swayed. "Hitch."

"What is he to you?" His words came out with tiny spaces between, a breath, no more, and it made her look at his face. What she'd taken for pain was anger, which surprised her.

"Sparks?" He nodded, and she tipped her head, unsure what he was truly asking. She decided to give him the truth. "He's... Ewell's my brother."

"Your brother?" His voice was laced with disbelief, so strong she was compelled to reassure him.

"Yeah, Sparks is my big brother." He chuckled, and she echoed it with a nervous laugh. "Why?"

"We're here." Rampage interrupted them as he paused before a wide set of doors.

She'd never noticed before, but the hallways and doors on this side of the clubhouse were all wider than normal for a house. Rampage had walked ahead of them, but if he'd needed to stay beside Hitch, he could have, with ease. Same for the door in front of them. Given she was pretty sure they'd had to carry Hitch inside when they arrived, she understood the reasoning. She didn't like it, but she understood.

Hitch's grip on her arm tightened as Rampage opened the doors.

The smell hit her first.

While the air conditioning had been turned full-blast in a clear effort to delay the inevitable process of death, it couldn't be halted, not in a crude morgue like this. Hitch made a guttural sound, and she sympathized with his distress. The three bodies rested on folding tables in the middle of the room. Talia was glad to see enough space had been left between the tables so she wouldn't have trouble moving around them to conduct her examinations.

She twisted her arm, intent on releasing herself, but found the strength of Hitch's grip unbreakable. He gazed at one of the dead men, expression distant while he stared fixedly at the body.

"Hitch?" His head jerked at her soft call, and his eyes swung to look at her. Wet with unshed tears, they were focused and pained. "I need to—" She didn't finish her explanation before he'd released her, flinging her wrist from him as if the connection burned him. "Are you okay?"

"No, I'm not." The muscles in his throat flexed and bunched as he swallowed hard. "I fuckin' am not. Never be again. Trammer's my brother, see? Those are my brothers, and it hurts like God's fist in my chest. But you got a job to do, and mine is to stay outta your way." He thumbed over his shoulder to the wall where chairs were drawn in a line. "I'll be over there. You need anything..." Hitch hesitated before he reached out and ran the backs of his knuckles down her cheek in a touch that was electric against her skin. "Just say the word, angel."

He made his way to a chair, unsteady on his feet. Hitch sat slowly, the movements carefully guarding his side, and she glanced at the bandage under his cut to find it still a pristine white. He was as well as she could make him, and given the arguments he'd ignored about taking it easy, he'd be as good as he allowed himself to be.

Taking a shallow breath, she turned away and faced those three tables again.

Time to get to work.

***

Talia

"What?" She startled and sat upright, palm scrubbing across her face as she blinked into Hitch's blue eyes. "Are you okay?"

He smiled, and that expression, plus the heat in his gaze, swirled all through her body, tingles running rampant along every inch of skin. She refused to glance down to see if her nipples were as hard as they felt, but from the attentive interest in Hitch's eyes, he'd already noted her reaction to him. *Every single time.*

"Yeah, Tee. I'm good."

Hitch had started calling her the nickname on the second day. The Jailbreakers were still on what Ewell called a lockdown, which basically meant everyone attached to the club was jammed into the limited number of available rooms. A few of the IMC members had stayed on-site too, including her uncooperative patient.

After their first joint trip up the hallway, he'd accompanied her everywhere he could between long, restful periods of sleep. His stride slow but steady, he'd trailed after her as he kept up his quiet but persistent questioning. Talia had no doubt that Hitch now possessed a full and thorough history of not only her but her family. The man was stubborn, and he was imbued with that certain breed of tough she'd only seen with Ewell and his men. She'd caught her brother watching them now and again, his expression always a mix of amusement and irritation.

Being around Hitch was no hardship, and she'd told herself it helped to keep an eye on her patient. It didn't matter what they were doing, Hitch made it better. Cutting up vegetables for dinner? He'd managed to tell a clean but suggestive story even the kids found amusing. Changing out his bandages? Depending on the audience, his stories were a lot more suggestive, and a lot less clean, but Talia found his crudeness wasn't a turnoff. *Not at all*.

"What do you need, Hitch?" She'd been curled up asleep on a big chair someone had pulled into her treatment room. Something poked her hip when she moved, and she realized it was the key her brother had given her. "How'd you get in?" *I know I locked that door.* She had meds in here, and security was second nature, even with her brother's men.

"It's dinnertime." He moved, and she saw a tray balanced on the exam table. "I brought you something to eat."

"That's sweet."

The door slammed open, rebounding against the wall. Hitch was between her and the door in a smooth movement, and she had to look around him to see Ewell in the doorframe.

"Talia." Ewell held his hand out commandingly. "Come on."

Hitch tightened his fingers around hers, and the tactile connection was the first realization Talia had that she was gripping his hand. She stepped up beside him, stopping when he applied pressure in his grip against the movement. Ewell and Hitch were locked into a staring contest.

"Hitch brought me some food." Hitch's fingers squeezed hers in response to her words. "Did you need me, Ewell?"

After another long, uncomfortable moment of silence between the two men, Ewell said, "Don't fuck up."

"Wha—"

"I won't." Hitch had cut her off with his answer.

Ewell looked at her finally, his expression fierce. "I fuckin' love you, little sis." Backing out, he slammed the door, the racket echoing in the small room.

Well if that's not the most confusing thing.

I Could be Persuaded

Hitch

It had only taken two days to find out who the cowardly bastards were who'd ambushed myself and my brothers. Pissed me off it took even that long. If I'd had more than half an unmuddled second to think, I could have come up with the name myself.

Vicar's Wrath, a longtime IMC enemy. They were the cosmic cockroaches of the club world, having been put down as an organization twice now, rebounding with fake patches and a faker brotherhood.

Dyno had shoved a chair my way earlier, his muttered message of "Talia" enough of a reason for me to accept it, and I sat forwards now, elbows to my knees as I stared at the images projected onto the screen.

I'd never realized the pain of being left behind. Even if necessary given my injuries, it hurt being cut out of the action I could see going down. I'd roped Dyno into running the command center from the back room of the Jailbreakers clubhouse, since both clubs were involved in our retaliation play.

We'd also hooked up with Myron, a tech genius from a northern tier club to which we had ties, and adding the Rebel Wayfarers assets behind ours meant even if I'd been relegated to the rear guard, I still got to watch and listen. Myron and Dyno had drones positioned around the farmhouse we'd identified as the Vicar's base of operations, with twelve camera views on a giant TV mounted to the wall.

Turned out Graceless had history with one of theirs, reaching more than a decade into the past. Took a black heart to hold onto bullshit for so long. As much as we'd like to just wipe them out, it was unlikely the entirety of their membership was culpable, so our targets had been isolated and identified using security footage from the liquor store. Every one of our brothers heading in had been thoroughly briefed on what to do if one of the eight were encountered. Yeah, theirs hadn't just been a surprise attack but also eight men against four, and one woman.

None of us had stood a chance.

Coming to the realization that, except for Graceless, the rest of us had been incidental damage felt weird.

I mean, come on. If I was going to be stabbed and shot, I wanted it to at least be because of something I'd done. *Assholes.*

There was abrupt movement on half the cameras, and I stared hard at the tiny squares of dark and bright. Heat signatures of bikes were coming down the drive towards the clubhouse. The other half of the cameras came to life as red and orange blobs—our men, my brothers—boiled out of the gloom surrounding the house.

An endless twenty minutes later, it was over. Thank God the numbers were in our favor this time, which meant we had exactly the result we'd wanted. Zero injuries on our side, and eight cancerous tumors surgically excised from their fake-as-fuck organization.

I leaned back in the chair and took in the view. On screen were our brothers. Standing around, back-slapping, and no doubt hooting loudly at the win. Standing, breathing—living.

"Is it over?" Talia's voice came a moment before her hand rested on my shoulder. I nodded, not saying anything, liking her touch too much. That same connection I'd felt before resonated through me at full strength, and I fought against leaning sideways so I could press up against her. This desire sweeping through me for more than her touch was unsettling. In my life I fucked and walked—I didn't do whatever this was. Still, I knew, after only these few days, she was necessary to me. Talia soothed me in ways I didn't recognize, couldn't put a name to if I'd tried, and goddamn I wanted her.

"Is everyone okay? Sparks?" Anger and unreasonable jealousy sliced through me at her murmured questions. Of course she wasn't here to check on me, wasn't here because she felt even a small part of this immense pull. She was here to check on her cockblocking brother.

The dry click of my swallow echoed in my ears. "Yeah, everyone's good." What I didn't say—and wouldn't voice to her—was that the eight cooling bodies would soon be carted out and placed into various vehicles, headed towards their final destinations. Listening to Dyno work through the logistics of disposal had been eye-opening—I'd never realized how much of his job was spent dealing with the aftermath of a confrontation like this. The man was a master. "Sparks is just there." I pointed to the lower right camera, showing Talia the yellow and orange of where he stood next to Twisted, bright red outlines of two men kneeling in front of them. "He's good."

Her relieved sigh had me feeling like an asshole about my flare of jealousy. *The man's her brother for God's sake.*

Talia moved, and I glanced to see her looking down at me, eyes narrowed. "How are you doing, Hitch?" I started to shrug and stopped when the pain woke in my side. "What would it take to get you to go to see a real doctor?"

"I thought you were a doc?" I was teasing, trying to lighten the mood, surprised at the dark look she shot my direction. "Kidding. I know you're a damn good EMT, and in my opinion, probably better than half the docs in the county." My borrowed wardrobe was comfortable, if unfamiliar, and I rubbed my fingers lightly over the shirt camouflaging the bandage around my middle. She'd changed it out every day, making sounds about the stab wound I still hadn't seen. "You did right by me, that's for sure."

"If you won't see a doc, then could I talk you into lying down somewhere and resting? If it's over, finally over, you can rest." Her palm pressed to my forehead was cool and glided like silk against my skin as she laid a soft touch against my cheek, then my neck. "You're hotter than you were before."

"That's what all the girls say," I teased, and her expressive face molded into a mask. "Hey," I said, reaching up to trap her hand against my face, "I kid." I flicked a gaze at the views from the cameras Dyno still had on the house and called out, "We're done here, right, Dyno?" He lifted a middle finger I took as my permission to withdraw. I studied Talia carefully as I bargained with her. "I'll go lie down if you rest with me. I heard from everyone how you've been working to take care of my ass. I'm a gentleman—" She snorted, and I faked shock at her reaction, happy to see her pretty mouth twist in an effort to keep from smiling. "I *am* a gentleman, and my health is important to me. As far as I'm concerned, it's still in your hands. I think it's only right you keep watch over me while I rest. I mean—" I forgot and tried again to shrug, wincing as the pain shot through me like a return of the blade.

"Dammit." After a careful breath in, I continued, "I mean, it's only right you make sure I'm going to be okay, right?"

Talia stared at me for a long minute, flicked her gaze to the screen where four men were now on their feet, signaling the beginning of the true end of the conflict, and looked back to me. She wavered visibly, tipped her head back as she rolled the muscles of her shoulders, and nodded. "Okay." Nose scrunched up, she shyly admitted, "I don't stay here, ever. I know a lot of the guys have rooms, but I don't. That's not me."

My chest swelled at her admission. In one fell swoop, she'd told me she didn't hook up with the club members and wasn't part of their day-to-day but was willing to change her ways. *For me.* "I got us covered." I reached up, and she took my hand, surprising me with her strength as she pulled me to my feet. I pretended to sway, and as I'd hoped, she stepped closer and wrapped one of those wiry arms around my waist. The heat of her blazed through me, burning away the last vestiges of my caution.

As we strolled up the hallway, I watched the expression on her face flicker from concern to uncertainty, and then inexplicably to sadness.

"Whatcha thinkin'?" My question made her glance up, a flash of her beautiful eyes before they were again downcast. "There's something goin' on in that smart noggin of yours. Share?" I steered us into the room where I'd been staying. Without releasing my arm from around her shoulders, I thumbed the lock after I closed it. "Spill, Talia. Confession is good for the soul."

Rolling her eyes at my lame attempt at humor, she tipped her head up and locked her gaze on me. "I envy

Ewell...Sparks. He's got this whole big family to lean on, something he built out of nothing."

"He's your family." I adjusted my hold so she stood in front of me. Arms around her waist, I gave her a squeeze. "You make it sound like you're alone. You're not. If there's anything I've learned about the man, it's that he'd do anything for you."

"Yeah." She gave me a half smile shaded by a hint of melancholy. "He's good like that."

"Nobody else around? No one waitin' on you to hie yourself home?" I was fishing and knew it, but she bit in a big way.

"Nope. I don't work again for another night, so no one to miss me." She blinked slowly and scoffed far back in her throat. "And doesn't that just sound like I'm whining? Sorry." My rigid grasp kept her from backing away, and her eyes lifted, our gazes meeting with an almost physical snap. "Hitch, let me go. I don't want to hurt you."

"You're not going to hurt me, Tee." I bent closer, moving slowly, giving her time to protest, willing to talk more if she needed. "You never could." Our faces were close enough that her every exhalation was a warm gust across my lips. "And there'll never be a time when I'll hurt you." Her hands rested against my chest, fingers fisting around the edges of my vest. "I never would."

Our lips met in the kind of soft caress we'd shared earlier, the sweetest glide of flesh on flesh as her chin tipped exactly as it should. She was the first to make a sound, a desperate moan of desire that set me on fire. I cradled her face in my hands, pulling her closer so I could devour her mouth, spearing my tongue between her lips to press deep. The decadent taste of her was the perfect mix of sweet and savory, instantly addictive as my tongue dueled with hers. She sucked hard, and I groaned down her throat, hips thrusting against her belly as my cock sought friction.

"Hitch." Her voice was scarcely louder than a breath, but I read all the need held inside her. That moan made a return as my hand fell to her breast, cupping and lifting, molding it to fit my hand as if she were made for me. "Tell me you feel this." I tweaked her nipple to make her gasp, that cool draw of air music to my ears. "Please, tell me I'm not alone," she begged, and I gave her my thigh to ride, fingers curled around her hip urging the primal movement she seemed to need.

"Fuck no, Tee. I'm right here with you. I've never wanted like this." I pulled back just enough to see her eyes. Pupils blown wide and black, the soft expression made her appear more vulnerable, and a swell of protectiveness rose within me. I needed her, full stop. "I wanna be in you, gotta watch you come apart, see what you look like when you come all over me. Gimme that, yeah? Let me have you." My dick throbbed, reminding me he was still locked behind my zipper. "We gotta hit the bed, baby. Clothes off, yeah?"

A flush rose from her chest through her throat and into her cheeks, turning her sun-kissed skin a deep rose as she nodded slowly. I kept hold of her with one hand while I tried my damnedest to work the fastening of my jeans with the other. Talia tsked softly and brushed my fingers away, dealing with it for me, the dance of her fingers so close to my cock the sweetest torture. There was one other critical thing to deal with before I could be truly comfortable.

Jeans hanging from my hips, I shrugged out of my vest, twitching it away from her when she would have taken it from me. Matching seams carefully, I smoothed and folded the leather before I set it aside. My brothers were avenged, and I'd been released from my vow. Talia seemed to understand this meant something and stood at my elbow until I finished.

She walked backwards towards the bed as she managed her own jeans, leading me with every step, showing me with each movement that this was her decision, too.

Clothing discarded on the floor, I made to follow her onto the bed and had to stifle a groan as the pain in my ribs woke. She must have seen it in my face, and her expression softened and shifted to concern. "I'm fine," I lied, then decided to offer up a morsel of truth when I told her, "but, things might go better if you're willin' to do all the work."

Talia stared at me, then dropped her head with a soft laugh. "This? All of this is against medical advice," she teased, then curled up on my good side as I lay on my back, a welcome presence I could get used to having. "But...I could be persuaded."

"Fuck yeah, I'll persuade the hell outta you," I muttered against the side of her head, shoving my arm underneath her neck to pull her closer. "Kiss me, gorgeous."

Intoxicated by the taste of her mouth, I kissed her while I stroked every inch of skin I could, memorizing each heady sound she made. Her hot palm wrapped around my cock, and the simple contact was overwhelming. I broke the kiss as I arched my neck, pushing my head into the cushioning pillow. "God damn, Tee."

She stroked down, then up, and the pad of her thumb swept across my piss slit, leaving pulses of heat behind. We set up a rhythm where on each tight and twisting downstroke, I thrust up into her grip until I was riding the edge of no return. With everything going on in the past few days, I wasn't sure I'd have any recovery if I blew my load now, so I had to stop her.

"Tee, get a condom, baby. My wallet." Fuck me if she didn't dip her head and bite my nipple, a place I hadn't realized was sensitive until that moment, the heat and pressure from her mouth making my hips jerk and chase her touch again. "Jee-sus," I drawled when she sucked hard. "Stop havin' fun like that, baby. Gonna get me off too soon."

"I wanna taste you," she told me, and good as her offer sounded, being inside her would be way better.

"No, baby. My Tee's goin' ridin' tonight." My shot and stitched arm protested as I wrapped my hand around hers, stopping her slow drag against my shaft. She tightened harder, and I grunted, then promised, "I can't do everything I want to you. Not right now. Not yet." Fighting my hold, she slipped down in the bed, mouth skipping over the bandage splitting me in two. "Dammit, baby." My good hand tangled in her hair and I stopped her mouth a bare breath from enveloping the head of my raging hard-on. "You're gonna ride me."

Faster than I expected, she caved, her agreement coming out in a softly drawn out, "Yeah," like she'd finally realized what I'd been saying.

I told her again, "Get a condom." Pointing towards my jeans with a tip of my head, I reminded her, "I got one in my wallet."

She scrambled off the bed, and fuck me if I didn't miss her heat immediately. Watching her move was nearly worth the loss, the sway of her back and arch of that fuckin' gorgeous ass definitely something I could get used to seeing. When she bent at the waist to fish the wallet from my jeans, I was presented with the prettiest hole shot I've ever seen, framed by her heart-shaped ass, with the soft curve of her plump pussy lips peeking out below. My mouth watered at the thought of getting my tongue and fingers into her everywhere. I must have made a noise, because her eyes found mine from around her legs and she grinned, telling me without words she'd posed just for me.

Talia straightened and turned to face me, fist pressed between her breasts. She said something, but I'd focused in on her tan nips, peaked and ready for my mouth. When she broke my field of view and covered those beauties with her arm, I looked into her face and muttered, "What?"

"Gah," she laughed. "*Men*. I said you have one."

She'd already lost me again, my gaze trailing down to where her bush hid the top of her pussy. Trimmed and tamed, but there, something I didn't know I liked until I saw hers done up like that. Club whores had been my only outlet for years, and they all shaved for ease of what-the-fuck-ever they did after the members partied with them. I could see her pink lips glistening between her legs and knew her sweet nectar would glide like silk against my tongue. *I want her so fuckin' bad.* Now my mouth was watering for sure, and I mentally revised the planned schedule of events for this encounter.

"Hitch." There was a tiny bite in her tone, and I brought my eyes back up to see she'd plastered a deep frown across her face. "Is your head worse? Are you with me?"

"Baby." I let my lips curl into a smirk. She stood naked, her body reacting to mine exactly like I wanted it to, but she was losing her happy place to worry about my damned head. The wrong one, I might add. "I'm good. It's just you're so fuckin' gorgeous I can't get my fill even starin' at you. Everything I see, I wanna touch and lick and bite, and your fuckin' pussy is callin' to me. I gotta taste you or I'm gonna go crazy. You're gonna ride my tongue before I get my dick in you. I wanna eat you out until you can't remember your own name."

Her smile was like a beam directed my way, bright and brilliant, and so fucking *there* it was all I could do to stay in that borrowed bed. I wanted to feel Talia's smile against my lips, wanted to ravish her mouth, wanted to kiss my woman until she could only think of me. I wanted to own that smile for myself, so she'd never give it to another man, ever again. *Just me*.

"Come here," I growled, stretching out my hand with a flick of my fingers. "Come right the fuck here."

She did, talking. "You've got one condom."

"Yeah?" Disappointing, but at least there'd been a rubber present. "Out of date?"

"Not quite" came with a partial beam, a tease of the full version, and my heart leaped at provoking even that from her. "It does look like it's been there a while."

"Yeah, I don't fuck around much." I wouldn't say never. It'd be a lie and one she'd sniff out in an instant. "Generally comes with drama and I ain't a fan." Climbing into the bed on her knees, she made her way back to my side. "So there's one. Is that a disappointment?"

"If this is the only time I get you, I guess I was hoping for a twofer at least." Talia's lips curled crookedly, and I lifted my chin in silent demand. She leaned close and brushed against my mouth, the heat and softness of her naked body draped across my shoulder making my dick take even more notice. "Then I remembered you're hurt."

"The condom's good for the main event." I watched as her beautiful eyes blinked open, pupils blown and dark again from our soft kiss. "I got lots of tricks up my sleeves to get you off without needin' more." Then I pushed. "This time." When her brow furrowed, I cut out the bullshit. "Ain't nothin' says this is it for us, Talia. I like you. There's just somethin' about you. Makes me a hella sap, because I've got all these things I want. I wanna fuck you, sure, but I wanna get to know you, too. I wanna make you happy, and not just in bed tonight. You feel like home, Talia, and I am gonna be back to explore that with you. Ain't a one-time thing for me, not in this bed, not with you. Even if I wanted to stay away, I doubt I'd manage. That's how strong whatever this is feels."

"After only a couple of days?" When she cupped my cheek, her fingers trembled, an endearingly unsteady touch against my skin.

"Yeah, Talia. After just the short time I've had with you, it's enough to know I want more." Arm curled around her waist, I gave her ass a squeeze, pulling her harder against my side. "What that more becomes, I don't know and won't lie to you just to get into your pants. Maybe outside of stressful events we're not compatible." Her lips pursed into a tiny moue, and I lifted my head to kiss the disappointment off her mouth. "I'm not expecting that as an outcome, darlin', just sayin'."

The glide of her fingers against my beard and skin was enough to fan the flames, and I glanced down to see my cock arching over my belly, a thread of shining fluid stretching down to where a pool was already gathered.

"You were basically unconscious the first time you kissed me."

"That wasn't a dream?" I knew it wasn't, and I remembered every moment of the kiss, but I wanted to see her smile. She didn't disappoint. "Damn, baby. Thought you were an angel come from on high to bring me back to life. Had to have me some of that."

"You surprised me." She laid her hand on my chest and traced a restless design there before pressing flat over my heart. I recognized it as an unconscious protective gesture, more evidence of our connection. "Covered in blood, and then you kissed me."

"And you—" I tipped her chin up as I raised my head, pressing my lips to hers, "—kissed me back."

"I..." She huffed a laugh at whatever was on her mind, then shared. "I wanted to know more about you from the instant I saw you get out of that van. You were obviously hurt, but something about you felt so vital. So alive. I guess I'm like you. I just wanted a little of that for myself."

"You got me, Tee." I tried to steer us out of the deep end and back to the fun I had planned. "Kiss me." Less a demand than I wanted, still it was the right direction. "Kiss me 'til we're both so fuckin' horny we can't wait another minute.

Then you're gonna ride my tongue." Her hips moved, and her bush was bristly against my thigh. "You're gonna plant that pretty pussy on my face and go to town and I'm gonna eat you out so good, baby. And then we'll put the single rubber to use. When your legs are jelly and my tongue's wore out, we'll ride some more."

The next little bit passed too fast for me. A blur of teeth and tongues, lips and groans, hands sweeping across bare flesh. Even from the bottom I battled for dominion, and she gave it to me, somehow gifting her submission while chasing my mouth. Soft and sweet, hard and fierce, every kiss rolled into another and lifted us higher. Fingers wound through her hair, I brought her mouth back to mine again and again, until I pulled harder, arching her neck to see her face, finding the love-drunk expression I'd been working for.

"Get up here," I ordered, and her eyes widened before she moved, scrambling up the bed to plant a knee on either side of my head, tucking her toes under my shoulders. I watched the show as she positioned herself, naked body arching backwards as she steadied herself with a hand on her knee. The expression on her face was excited and turned on, but still a tiny bit hesitant. "You're not gonna break me, baby." Waggling my tongue at the promise of her only inches above my mouth. "Gimme." My demand made her smile. "Hold yourself open with one hand, Tee. Use the other to show me what you want. Don't be afraid to pull me closer. I wanna know what you need."

Mouth open, panting, she did just that. Two fingers separated her pussy lips to show me the bounty I was looking forward to, and her other hand curled behind my head, nails scratching gently at my scalp. My one arm wasn't good for anything in this position, but I grabbed her ass with the other and yanked her down the final distance separating us until I had my mouth on her. Slick and wet, and so fucking sweet I couldn't believe how she tasted.

Diddling her pearl had her humping my face with a cry, gliding those wet lips so my tongue could circle her entrance before plunging in. And the sounds she made. Damn, I didn't know that'd be a turn-on for me, but my rock-hard cock throbbed painfully with every sigh, jerked with each stifled moan, and slapped my belly when I found a particularly good angle so she whimpered. Her voice dipped low to say my name, then found a higher register as she called me a god.

I wrapped my fingers around the top of her thigh, playing until I found her clit with a fingertip and thrummed it side to side while I fucked her deep with my tongue and got her off for what might have been the third time. Her legs stiffened and lifted, and I chased her pussy with help, the hand she had gripping the back of my head holding my mouth tight against her. The rising wail of her orgasm filled the room, and I couldn't wait anymore, didn't want to, didn't give a shit if she was still coming, I needed her on my dick now.

"Slide down, baby." My words didn't pierce the veil of her pleasure, so I lapped at her another dozen times. "Talia." That got me her eyes, hooded and dark in her flushed and sweaty face.

She licked her lips, and asked, "Yeah?"

"Ride my cock."

Another glide of her pink tongue across those bitten-red lips and she nodded.

I gave her clit a final fierce suck as she bucked her sleek sweetness against my face, then gently bit the inside of her thigh. "Now, baby. I need you."

She was positioned over my dick before I remembered. "Condom. Where'd it go?"

"I don't know." Her breathy answer was nearly a sob and she wrapped her fingers around my cock, stroking up as she slid to straddle my thighs. "Where?"

The flash of the wrapper caught my eye, and I jerked my chin in that direction. Problem solved, she smoothed the raincoat down my shaft with a gentle touch, pinching the top like a good girl.

We'd been playing so long that when she seated herself on my cock, I lost it. It was so unbelievably good to be inside her heat, to feel her pussy clasping my shaft, force her open, that slick channel parting before my thrusts, I became wild. My words, my breath, even the thoughts in my head had slipped away. Everything was fucking gone, and the only thing remaining was a man desperate to fuck his woman.

Pain be damned, my hands were in a tight hold around her waist as I dug my heels into the mattress and yanked her down so the sweet curves of her ass rested against my thighs, and I was finally—fucking finally—balls deep. I froze there, surfacing from the mania, searching her face, afraid to see pain and anger there. Instead, what I saw was the sultry expression of a woman who liked what she'd gotten so far and was waiting and ready for what came next.

Pumping experimentally, I found a range of movement that worked for the wound and bruising in my side. Nothing would be completely comfortable, but God damn, this woman was worth any pain. *Anything*. Talia's fingers curled around the back of my neck as she brought her titty to my mouth, letting me tongue and play with the beaded beauty of her lush nipple before I sucked hard, making her moan softly. Another slow thrust and her head rolled backwards, exposing the delicate column of her throat, marked by my mouth from earlier. The satisfaction and possession that swept over me was surprising, and I tucked those thoughts aside, giving my dick full rein.

I held a rigid position as I swatted her ass, an encouragement to keep her moving on top of me. The long muscles in her thighs tightened and bunched as she rose and fell, using my hips as her launching point. We both worked up a sweat, turning the glide of her skin across mine into a delicious treat, nearly as mind-blowing as the way her sweet pussy clamped down on my cock, pulling and sucking me deeper. Talia's ass slapped my thighs, and I grabbed a handful on each side, tugging in time with her rhythm of taking me deep, encouraging more of that delicious slide and glide.

She leaned over me, ass moving in a pattern only she understood. Her mouth latched onto my pec again, teeth digging deep, and the unexpected burst of erotic pain had me groaning her name. She lifted and stared at me, mouth wet and swollen, her damned beautiful eyes dark and lust-filled. I wrapped my fingers in her hair and brought her in for a kiss broken only by our panting breaths. It ended with her forehead pressed to mine, and I watched as she came apart. Her pussy walls clutched me, drawing me deep as I hammered up into her, balls tight against my body. Muscles tensed with the electric spasms racking her she cried out once, then again, and then it was me who was gone, fucking gone, driving towards my own orgasm. Tight and wet, her pussy took every thrust, magnifying the sensation of being inside someone to another level.

It wasn't just someone taking my cock. It was Talia. And knowing, feeling, believing she'd wanted this as badly as I did sent me over the moon.

***

Talia

Hitch cried out as his body arched up and Talia gripped his shoulder to keep from being dislodged. She'd scarcely come down from her orgasm, the climax seeming to last forever with the thick shaft of Hitch's cock drilling into her. He'd angled his hips perfectly to glide his dick in ways that'd roused a burning fire in her belly, catching hold and setting her ablaze. Now she got to see him in the throes of his own ecstasy, and he was gorgeous as he unraveled underneath her.

Mouth open, his jaw moved, lips forming her name over and over, tongue dipping out to glide across his bottom lip. He righted his head, eyes opening and focusing immediately on her face, an expression of satisfaction coming over him at whatever he saw there.

"Kiss me, beautiful." He pursed his lips in an example of what he wanted, and she obliged, dipping low to press her mouth to his. "Goddamn," he muttered, the movement of his lips sexy as hell before he distracted her by gliding his tongue in a slow dance against hers. "Fuckin' me like that. Takin' my cock. Lettin' me have you." Each phrase was punctuated with another deep kiss as they caught their breath. "Gonna hafta—" He growled and kissed her hard, the biting edges of his teeth and brutal thrust of his tongue making her gasp into his mouth. "Keep you."

His hand slipped up her back and cradled the back of her neck, a hold he used to bring her down so she was lying on top of him, head tucked underneath his chin while his other arm wrapped around her waist. "I should move," she told him, surprised when her protest stirred another slow thrust of his scarcely softened cock into her. "Stop," she scolded, but knew it held no heat when he chuckled, the rumbling movement of his chest comforting.

"Like you right where you're at, woman. You try to move now, I'ma smack that ass." His arm gave her a squeeze she welcomed, granting silent permission to relax in place. "Lemme bliss out for another couple of minutes, Tee. This right here? This is fuckin' worth everything."

She rested on him while he stroked and petted her back and side, the movements coming slower with each pass.

"It's nearly the best part of everything." She spoke quietly, listening to his unhurried, even breaths in and out. Regular and steady, the sound was as comforting as those of waves against a beach. His grip on her waist eased, his hand coming to rest on her bent knee at his hip. "Just being." The heaviness of his breathing deepened, sound coarsening as he drifted to sleep.

Once he was well and truly at rest, she slipped off him, careful to hold the condom in place on his soft cock until she'd disengaged. Rooting around in the adjoining bathroom, she uncovered a washcloth and soap, using them to clean herself before going back to stand next to the bed. Hitch lay on his back, head angled so one cheek was against the pillowcase. His good arm had wrapped across his chest, hand tucked on top of the bandages she was glad to see unstained with blood. At least their ill-advised activities hadn't broken open his wound.

She thoroughly wiped him down, impersonally holding his penis as she did so, lifting his scrotum to gently swipe at the sweat she knew would have collected on his perineum. When he groaned and arched into her touch, she glanced up to see a tortured expression on his face, tiny lines fanning from the corners of his tightly closed eyes. His lip lifted, and she prepared for a shout or expletive, but what ground from his mouth wasn't that. Just her name, spoken in a broken plea, "Talia."

Discarding the cloth in the bathroom, she studied herself in the mirror. Tousled hair, lips red and roughened from his beard, love bites dotting her dusky skin—she looked well fucked. Then she remembered how she had felt in his arms, nestled against his chest. Cherished by a proud man willing to take a more passive role than he was clearly accustomed to if it meant they could be together for another minute.

She flipped off the light, padding through the darkness to climb back into bed with Hitch.

Her heart leaped when he reached for her without fully waking, curling around her protectively, ever the bossy man, ordering her to "Sleep" with a gruff word before he relaxed into her.

She complied, dozing off with his welcome weight pinning her to the mattress.

Paradise Found

Hitch

I woke slowly, drifting up from the deep sleep that had held me in its grip for hours. There was this immense sense of peace in my chest. Not something I was accustomed to, and I spent a few brain cells trying to sort it out before the heat of a body next to mine registered. *Talia.* I'd know her scent or the feel of her anywhere. She was not beside me. I'd sprawled out over her until the woman lay plastered to the bed.

Thoughts of the previous night swept through my head. They provided a vivid stop-action film of our activities that had my cock soaking up the memories like a sponge, fattening and uncoiling from where it rested against the small of Talia's back.

When I tried to shift to the side, the aftermath of the other events came crashing back in, reminding me I'd very nearly been dead at one point in the past couple of days.

Still, it was worth it to hear my angel's voice. "Hitch?" Soft and sleepy, she asked, "You okay?"

"Yeah, baby." I rested against her, teasing flawless skin with my teeth, then pressed a kiss there. "With you here? I'm fuckin' great. Tip-top." My chest aborted a cough before it made it to a full-fledged hack, while the resulting sharp movements made me hiss and groan. "Fuck, Jesus. What the hell?"

"You were shot," Talia helpfully reminded me, rolling out from underneath me. Hair in a tangle around her head, clasped fists curled beneath her chin, she offered a wry look. "And stabbed."

"And beaten." I couldn't argue with her assessment. "Still sucks. I woke up with plans for ya. All the plans." The stitches in my arm pulled when I lifted my hand, and I ignored the pinch of pain, counting it necessary if it meant I got to touch her.

"So many plans?" Lips lifting unevenly, she gave me a twisted grin as she pressed into the caress. "All the plans?"

"Yeah, baby, all those motherfuckin' plans." The apple of her cheek fit my hand, just like her body had fit mine last night. We were matched in every way, and my resolve from the preceding day returned. "I'm keepin' you. You know that, right?"

Talia rolled her lips between her teeth, biting down for a moment. "I live here in Adkins."

"So? That's not some magical barrier to me keepin' you, babe. That's a tiny wrinkle, not a shut and locked door. You like livin' here? Grew up here? Wanna stay here where you're close to your brother?" She gave the tiniest of nods to each question, answering each individually. "You wanna 'xplore this with me?" Another nod, larger than the others. "Wanna keep me around?" I got a grin and a solid dip of her chin to her neck, lashes fluttering to hide her eyes. "Then I'll sort my shit and figure out what it means for me."

Her gaze darted to my face, dancing between my eyes as I gave her a minute to consider what it all meant. It didn't take long before she was rolling her lips again, biting them nervously.

"What, Talia?" I shoved my other hand underneath her head, cradling her face between my palms as I drew her closer. Our noses brushed, and the heat of her breath swept over me as I asked again, "What's goin' on in that noggin, beautiful? I'm not a man to wait around. When I want something, I take it. I want you. Means a change in my life, I'm down with it. It'd be worth anything to wake up to you like this every fuckin' day. Bottom of my heart, I mean that."

Trembling lips parted, and the flash of her tongue peeked out. Then she rocked my world.

"I could love you."

"Oh, baby," I ground out, pressing her face to my throat while I buried myself in her hair. After a moment, I shoved up on an elbow and stared down at her. "If you're gonna give me all that beauty inside you all at once, I'm gonna overdose on the sweet. You could love me?" She nodded, and I busted her lips free from her teeth, taking her mouth in a deep, wet slide, drinking my fill from her. When I broke the kiss, she blinked up at me with an expression fast becoming my favorite. Love-drunk and aroused looked gorgeous on her.

"Every day I'll work to be worthy." Her lashes drifted to touch her cheeks, and I saw the muscles in her throat tighten as she swallowed hard. What I was saying meant something to her, a deep and profound emotion playing across her features when she opened her eyes to stare up into my face. "I wanna be worthy. Wanna be everything for you."

Talia lifted to meet my mouth, and I chased her lips until she was panting and writhing and my dick was hard enough to pound nails.

A knock at the door had me groaning as I whipped my head around to glare at the blameless surface.

"Yeah?"

"You still alive in there, Hitch?" Twisted's voice came through the wood, concern and amusement constant bedfellows in his tone. "Brother, it's time we hit the road. Gonna hafta say goodbye to the pretty chickie."

Another voice joined his. "Talia Rosalie, are you in there?"

Talia groaned and covered her face with both hands.

"Jesus, Sparks," I called out, pulling Talia closer, puffing up when she buried her face against my chest. *I'll protect her against anything comin' our way.* "Wanna back the fuck off my woman?"

There was silence, and when Talia drew back, I found myself smiling down at her shocked expression. "You misplace the knowledge that I'm keepin' you?" She shook her head in a slow side-to-side arc. "By definition that makes you my woman."

"That's my brother."

"So? Right now, him and my national president are both"—I raised my voice to project to our visitors—"unwelcome as fuck, pullin' this shit." Laughter from the hallway told me my words weren't taken the wrong way, giving me freedom to push a little more. In the sternest voice I could muster from around my grin, I ordered them, "Go. Away."

"Talk in fifteen," Twisted insisted, and I had to grunt in annoyance at the proof my president and friend was an asshole determined to cockblock me this morning. "You get me, Hitch?"

"Oh yeah. I fuckin' get you, boss." Ignoring the sounds of leave-taking from behind the door, I dragged my thumb across Talia's lips, reiterating the important part of what he'd said. "Fifteen."

Adjusting my position along her side, I held her in place when Talia would have pulled away. "Hitch, we've got to get up."

"I've got—" I kissed her, softly in the beginning, ramping up into a scorching joining of lips and breath, pushing until she had that dazed expression on her face again. "Fifteen minutes to teach you what's going to happen every morning from here on out." Forehead fitted against hers, I brushed the tips of our noses together.

No longer banished to no man's land, I'd somehow found myself in a paradise I could hold on to.

"Keepin' you," I reminded her.

"Lettin' you," she rejoined, and I smiled against her lips.

"Fuck yeah."

***

Talia

She was straightening her treatment room, itemizing the various replacement supplies she needed Ewell to pick up, when she heard shouts coming from the clubhouse office. The words were indistinct at first, but when she stuck her head out the door, everything came clear.

Hitch was having the conversation he'd promised Twisted and Ewell, but it didn't sound as if it were going in a direction any of them were pleased with.

"No. Fucking no." That was Hitch, followed by indistinct murmuring from Ewell.

"Yes, you fuckin' will." Even from the few times she'd heard him speaking, Twisted's voice was unmistakable. "Just because we've neutralized one pit of vipers don't mean we've killed the nest. Even bodiless heads can still bite and poison a person. We need you, brother."

"You don't fuckin' understand, man. I'm not leaving her behind."

Talia's heart skipped a beat, pain curling deep behind her breasts.

"I'm not letting you put her at risk. Not happening." Ewell's bellow shook the windows in their frames. "Your shit is *not* sorted, man. Unsorted shit can seep, and I've got enough challenges keeping just my shit away from my baby sister. Don't add yours, man."

"Take a breath, darlin'."

Talia whirled, straightening as she stared at Rampage. He'd come up the hallway behind her and was looking at her with sad understanding in his gaze.

"He's going to have to leave, isn't he?" She already knew the answer to her own question, because officer or not, club members didn't buck their president. If Ewell said something when acting as Sparks, his men would break themselves in half to make it happen. Hitch couldn't be anything except the same kind of man. *Loyal to a fault.* "If it's what Twisted wants, he won't have a choice."

"Never saw the man act like he does around you."

Talia shook her head, blinking as she tried to make sense of what Rampage had told her. "What?"

"Hitch. Never seen him like this. You're under his skin, pretty lady. If you're worried about him making a return trip to see you, I'd say it's pretty much a given." Arms out, he took a step towards her, and Talia backed into her treatment room. Rampage herded her farther inside, then leaned forwards and gripped the doorknob. He closed the door on his final words. "Man's a goner for you. He's given you something he never gave anyone else. Not even Trammer. You gonna keep it safe?"

There was a click, and then she was alone with the blameless blank surface of the door staring back at her. "Keep it safe" twined around inside her head with what Hitch had told her last night, then reminded her this morning: "keepin' you." What Rampage was asking should have been just an expanded version of the other, but it felt like so much more.

A thudding impact against the wall in front of her rocked Talia back on her heels. She watched as the surface shivered; then the door was ripped open and Hitch stood there. A fresh bruise spread along his jaw, and she saw the restlessly clenching knuckles of one hand were shredded. A commotion rolled up the hallway to where he stood, but he didn't look back at the noises, kept his eyes on her as he stepped towards where she waited, crowding close, heat from his body spreading along her front.

"Talia." That was it, just her name, but somehow she understood everything he tried to convey.

"It's okay." She pressed her palm against his chest—not to hold him back, which would have been impossible—but to remind herself of the most important thing in all their story so far. The rapid beat of his heart soothed her, letting her successfully blink the tears away. *He's alive.* "I'll be waiting."

"*Fuck.*" The growled word split the air around them, raining pain down on her skin until she shivered in his arms. "It'll just be a little while."

She turned her face and offered him her lips, something he took her up on immediately. Hitch fit his mouth against hers, sipping delicately with tiny kisses, each a bare press and release that lit her on fire from within but did nothing to assuage the blaze. On his next pass, she darted her tongue out to swipe at his lips, undoing some of his control, because he groaned into her mouth. The taste of Hitch flooded through her as he stroked against her tongue, licking and nibbling.

"I'll be waiting." She held tight to her promise. "I'll be here."

Take the Fight to Them

Hitch

Arguably the hardest thing I'd ever done was climbing on my bike and riding away, watching my woman dwindle to nothing in my rearview. She'd said all the right things, and I'd watched closely enough to ensure it wasn't an act. In the end, my national president had won the day because my ass was on my bike, in a column behind him, and she wasn't with me.

All the things he and Ragman had said made sense; they just burned painfully to hear. We were at war. No way to get around that statement, because our hit on their clubhouse might not have been the opening salvo, but it for sure wasn't the final one, either.

The cartel sponsoring the piece-of-shit club that'd been built on the bones of old ruins hadn't backed down. Last night, while I'd been sleeping with Talia—hours after we cleared the vipers from that fucking clubhouse across the state—we'd received a clear message in the delivery of the head of one of our own.

It wasn't a member I knew well, but I knew him. He was what we referred to as fodder. Not a strategist to help mold policy or events, not an out-front leader, or even a behind-the-scenes mover-and-shaker—he'd been the kind of man who'd stand firmly shoulder to shoulder with his brothers. The ones who held the line, lending strength to the men next to them, and the next. The note found in his mouth had been not a taunt, but a threat, stating: "You did this. Every member bears responsibility."

Ragman had tipped the scales for me this morning, making his play in a way he knew I wouldn't turn down.

"Cartel's already dropped a list, man."

I pinned him in place with my gaze, because I knew exactly what he meant by those few words. The Mexican drug cartels had migrated to social media nearly as fast as the jihadists, utilizing the pervasive nature of the software platforms as a way to get into everyone's pocket. Nearly every enemy and friend had smartphones, and nearly all those phones had one platform or another.

"You wanna share the names on that list, Rags?" A list meant a death sentence for every single person recorded. It was being put on notice, told to get affairs in order, because as far as the cartel was concerned, you were already pushing up daisies. "Anyone we know?"

"Your name might have shown up on a few." Ragman didn't shift his gaze away from me, even when Twisted made a pained noise. "Along with every other officer the

IMC fields. Officers—and their families. But as of right now, it appears the Jailbreakers have coasted under the radar. Our goal is to keep it that way."

What he hadn't said, hadn't needed to put to words, was the fact that if the role Sparks and his Jailbreakers had played in our retaliation landed them in the cartel's rumor mill, anyone and everyone attached to them would be in danger. Including my Talia.

So, when I was told to pack my shit and get, I first found Talia and talked, finding her surprisingly easy to convince. That in itself was suspect at first, and I imagined it was her giving me an out, which pissed me right the fuck off.

I was wrong, but me tearing my stitches while fucking the idea clean out of her head pissed her off.

I counted myself the winner anyway. Angry sex was good sex.

My gaze flicked to my mirror, automatically cataloging the men behind me. The pain in my gut hit hard when I realized I was looking for Trammer and not finding him. *Not ever gonna find him again.* "Fuck."

Forcing my thoughts away from the losses and back to Talia, I remembered with pride how she'd held her head high, chin lifted as we said goodbye. I couldn't tell her the why of everything, and I loved the fact she didn't cling, just kissed me with everything inside her and backed away as I settled onto the bike. The way the driveway around the Jailbreakers' clubhouse curved, I could keep my eyes on her until we rolled off the gravel and onto the highway. Head on a swivel, I kept my gaze locked on her face and she held that damned smile for me until I couldn't see her anymore.

I'll be back. I repeated my promise to her over and over in my head. *I'll be back real soon.*

Eyes fixed in front of me, I rode the remaining miles at speed, following the club's leadership in more than a symbolic way, hoping we could find a quick end to this.

We pulled into Mother's clubhouse, and I'd be the first to admit I wasn't prepared. They'd brought brothers to the Jailbreakers house for the tactical assault, and I'd felt the grief from them. We were only days away from losing Trammer, Graceless, and Pizzaboy, and I'd been neck-deep from the get-go, but it wouldn't have occurred to me that I had an advantage over anyone.

I did.

Their deaths had been a visceral awakening for me. I understood the gaping wound left inside me—inside and out. As it should be when every waking moment, and some of my sleeping ones, had been spent processing what had happened.

The dozens upon dozens of men standing on the clubhouse grounds in front of me hadn't made it as far along the road as I had. Not leaving my brothers behind, never that, but moving along to where their memories were not always painful.

They were on me before I finished getting my kickstand down.

Man after man, a seemingly endless line of grief I had to battle through, hearing the muttered curses as my brothers grabbed tight to what remained. Me.

After the last member approached me, I looked up to see Twisted standing on the front porch, feet wide apart, fists propped on his hips. He stared at me for a long minute, then called me up beside him with a brusque tip of his head. I took the steep stairs slowly, one foot in front of the other until I was next to him. He shocked me by doing exactly what the other members had done, drawing me into a one-armed clinch and pounding my back gently. Mouth to my ear, he told me, "The club continues, as it should. IMC isn't dependent on one single member but the sum of it all. You takin' their grief on like you did tonight, you've welded that entity even tighter together. Proud of you, brother."

I had no words, nothing I could say that was pithy or wise. All I had was pain and exhaustion, and more anger than I expected because I'd been made to leave Talia behind. Just because it made sense didn't mean I liked it. At all.

Voice soft, pitched just for my ears, with every word spoken Twisted proved he understood exactly where I stood. "War ain't pretty. When you turn around and look at the men standing at our backs, you mark the fact that three in ten likely will not be there at the end of things. Thirty percent, brother. Those are men who've vowed to protect with vigorous application of will. For the most part, they understand what we're facing—and what they don't get right now, we'll clear up by the end of the night. Not a one of us is innocent. Our women and children, though? For them, their man is primary, and anything to do with the club is secondary. That is as it should be, too. Talia couldn't be here standing next to you. And won't be, not until we clear our patch of ground from this threat."

"Will we ever, though?" I hadn't meant to respond to him, but his words resonated with me, except that last portion. "Won't it be another threat following, and another?"

"None like this one, man. Not for you. They've taken it personal-like."

I nodded and stepped back, studying Twisted's face. He looked tired, and strained, but there in those warm brown eyes was still the spark of confidence I needed to see.

"Then we take the fight to them." I lifted my lip, curling it arrogantly. "Personal-like."

Pain and Darkness

Talia

Working helped, she found. Even the monotony of sitting in the ambulance waiting for a call was better than lying in her own bed staring into the darkness.

He'd been gone three days before she got the first call. Seeing an unknown number, she'd thumbed her phone to silent mode and let it go to voice mail, only listening to the message after she'd finished her shift.

"Hey, baby." Even now her eyes drifted closed at the memory of his low, vibrato voice in her ear. "Gotta use a burner for now, but it should be safe for me to call and text this way. Two rules, though. You don't call back, because I'll be yankin' the battery soon as I hang up. So don't call back, ever. And second, you lose my real number. Delete it now, so you can tell me you did it when we connect. I got my reasons, and ain't one of them gonna be what you might be thinking, so get those thoughts out of your head." He'd paused a moment, and she'd heard him pull in a breath that sounded painful somehow. "Keepin' you. Remember that, through everything that might come our way. *I'm. Keeping. You.*"

It had been another two days before he'd called back, and she'd nearly fallen over herself in her rush to answer the phone, the need to hear his voice a primal craving strumming through her body. She didn't try to decide what it meant, just accepted it as part and parcel of this thing between them.

Short but sweet, the call had underscored her hope and desire to build something with him. He'd again talked about relocating if she didn't want to leave Ewell but put a caveat on it this time. "After this shit's done, you and me are gonna take one hell of a trip. You on the back of my bike, we'll take to the road, decide where to go turn by turn. Just you and me, you got me? Will you do that with me, Tee? Can you give me that to look forward to?"

It had felt like he needed the promise, because he'd pushed until she'd given it to him. "Anything you want, Hitch. I'll be there, at your back."

Any hesitation she'd felt had disappeared when he'd responded immediately. "Give me what I need, every fuckin' time. That's my baby. Right back atcha, baby. You speak a need, trust that you're speakin' it into existence, because I'll fuckin' meet it. That's my goddamned promise to you, Tee. I'll meet it."

In the month since, they'd talked every few days. Nothing like a set schedule, but he'd clearly memorized her shifts and usually called after she'd had a chance to get home. She'd unlock the door, put on the hands-free headset, and cook supper, do laundry, clean, or work out. She'd wait.

On the days he did call, she'd quickly gotten used to their rhythm. They'd chat a bit about her work, about Ewell, about her house, until Hitch would start to tease her. He'd mention he was lying in bed, wishing she was there, and that would start the fun times. She'd never known phone sex could be that satisfying.

"Talia."

She jerked upright, suddenly aware she'd been drifting in her head for a while.

Looking to her left, she saw her partner frowning at her. Again. This had become a common occurrence in the past few days.

"Yeah?"

"I asked if you wanted to go out after our shift. There's a few of the guys headed to the bar." He made a show of checking his watch, even though there was a clock embedded in the dashboard. "We got a half hour until we're done, and it's been—"

She lunged across the space separating them, slapping her hand across his mouth. "Shut it. Do not jinx us."

He rolled his eyes, laughing as he shook off her hand. "Superstitious."

"It's true and you know it." She made big, shocked eyes at him. "You know it as well as I do. Saying what you were about to say ensures Mother Karma pays attention."

The radio crackled, the sound of their dispatcher keying a previously silent mic, and she glared at him even more while they waited. Nothing else came through, and Talia huffed a breath of relief while he laughed.

After a few minutes, she remembered the question that had started their exchange. "No bar for me tonight. I gotta go home and wash my hair."

He grinned and looked out the side window, shaking his head. "Whatever, Talia. What ev-ah."

The phone in her back pocket buzzed, and she scrambled to pull it out. The display said Unknown Number, and her heart raced as she glanced at her partner. *Hitch*. "I gotta take this."

She already had the door opened and was climbing out by the time he replied, a nonsensical response that had her staring at him as the phone rang again. "I'm sorry."

Phone to her ear, she waited for Hitch's usual greeting but instead heard only dead air. She looked at the screen as she slammed the ambulance door. Turning away, she struggled to stifle the overwhelming feeling of loss at missing the call. Then she realized the call timer was ticking up, as if it were still connected. Lifting the phone again, she queried, "Hello? Hitch?"

"No, *senorita*. Guess again." The oily, deep voice was heavily accented, and the call had an odd echoing effect, as if she were hearing the words twice, slightly delayed.

"What?" A car blasting past honked its horn, and she also heard it twice, slightly delayed.

Talia jerked the phone away from her ear, scanning the area around where the ambulance was parked as she stabbed the button to disconnect the call. A shadow separated from the dimness within a nearby alley and began moving her way. Talia reached behind her for the door handle, shocked when her hand hit only open air. She whirled in time to see the vehicle bounce across the curb, gaining speed as it pulled into traffic and drove away. For just a moment, her partner's silhouette was in view, but he looked steadfastly forwards, not once glancing back to where he'd left her. She had only partially turned back to face the shadowy man when pain blasted through her neck, turning her muscles into rigid blocks of flesh.

The sidewalk rushed up at her, unforgiving as she landed on the concrete face-first, not even able to lift her hands to break her fall.

Black boots with square scuffed toes appeared in view, stepping close to her face. She heard a vicious crackling of electricity right beside her ear. Flinching didn't help, her muscles still locked tight. The sound seemed to go on forever, until the pain and darkness swallowed her up.

Go On From Here

Hitch

"No, man. She's not answering." I answered Sparks' question impatiently. "She always picks up. Don't matter when or where, my woman picks up."

Sparks made a pained sound, a grumpy noise I knew was due to my claiming statement. I needed the man to get past his desire to protect Talia from whatever it was he thought I represented. *Now*.

"Sparks," I started, closing my eyes to focus more fully on the call. In an instant, I decided to lay myself out before the man, because that'd be the only way he'd be able to trust me. "She's it for me, and I can't say it any plainer than that. She's it from A to Z and back again. Got a power over me with each word from her mouth. I want...no, I need to know she's okay, because from where I stand right now, I can't do or even think about anything else, man. I'm keepin' her." I pulled in a breath, not trying to hide how shaky it was. "Now, right now...I gotta know she's okay. If she's not at your clubhouse, and she didn't pick up for you"—something I knew because he'd already disclosed the fact—"then I'm askin' you to send someone to her place, to check on her. She's not on shift tonight and should be home."

"I got someone rollin' already."

I couldn't find any anger in me for the knowledge he had been busting my balls, only an easing of the tightness that had been choking me for the past few hours as I tried and failed to contact Talia.

"Obliged, man. Call me as soon as you know anything? Use this number." I rattled it off, since I'd dialed him from the burner, not that he'd know that fact since there was no reason for him to have my regular number.

After getting a grunt that I hoped like hell signaled compliance, I disconnected the call with my thumb and stared across the table at Twisted. He was shaking his head slowly, the pained expression on his face foreshadowing what he was about to say. I cut him off with a gesture. "No, not until I hear back from him. I don't wanna hear it, brother. I can't hear it. You get me?"

Ragman stepped up beside me and rested an arm across my shoulders. He gave me a squeeze for a moment, then dropped his hold and continued across the room to stare out the window.

"Any progress on tying that group down in Homer to this bunch?" Twisted's question seemed to come out of left field, and I wasn't the only man in the room who looked at him with a sideways-tilted head.

"Not that I'm aware of." Ragman didn't turn around, making his statement as if addressing the clear glass in front of him.

"How about figuring out where they post this shit from?" Twisted turned to face the rolling board we'd been using to pin and write information on, trying to draw lines between what seemed like a sea of unassociated things. "I'm not above involving other clubs, long as they know what they're stepping into. So if we haven't talked to Mason yet about what Myron might can do for us, then let's make that call now while we're waitin' on Sparks to get back to us."

I stared around the room to find all faces turned to me. Rolling my neck, I laid the burner on the table and got out my phone. Looking up the number took only seconds, and within a few moments from that, the conference phone was echoing with the ringing tones of a call waiting to be connected. Twisted gestured brusquely and most of the men who'd been crowding around the room quietly filed out.

There was a cautious "Hello," but before I could respond, it was followed by the sound of a blow, not quite fist on flesh. I stared at Twisted, who was shaking his head back and forth again but this time had an amused smile on his face. A moment later, another voice came on the line. This one I recognized. "The fuck IMC want? What the hell you doin' callin' this time of the goddamned morning?"

"And a good day to you, too, Gunny." The man's grunt made me smirk, giving away the fact that he didn't like being recognized so easily. "IMC would like to have a conversation with Mason, if you please."

"Mason, or the national president?" That was a fair question, because it would mandate the kind of protocol we'd have to follow for this call. I glanced at Twisted, who looked like he'd sucked on a lemon, mouth pulled to one side.

"Nat prez." Twisted gritted the words out as he looked at me with shuttered eyes, all emotion driven away. "No way around that shit, man."

"In that case, give me a minute to transfer the call." Gunny had evidently recognized Twisted's voice, because he didn't ask if the person on the call had the standing to make this kind of request for our club.

There was a click and hum, and I opened my mouth, only to close it when Twisted lifted a finger. We stood in silence until there was another click, followed by the murmuring of several men. I could only make out snatches of conversations, but it sounded just like casual chatter that went on in every meeting just before it was called to order. We waited, and finally we heard the voice we'd wanted.

"IMC, I understand we've got Twisted there. Care to enlighten us as to who else we're talking to?"

Twisted inclined his head, which I took as my permission to speak now. "On this end we've got Twisted, Ragman, and Hitch. Appreciate you takin' the call, Mason."

"My sister's man's club calls, I fuckin' pick up." He was talking about Justine, his sister who'd moved to Mandeville recently from Adkins, Florida. She was the reason the RWMC was connected to Sparks' club, the Jailbreakers, because Mason had reached out more than once to have Sparks and his brothers provide assistance when it involved his sister. Then she'd gotten herself into a world of hurt and been rescued by IMC, resulting in her hooking her star to our own Wildman. "On this side, you lucked out with your timing. We hadn't yet shut the doors, but we were close, so you got every fuckin' officer in the Fort, along with some nationals down from Chicago."

That meant they'd called church, but at an odd time of day, since like most clubs, they'd typically do an officer meeting in the evening, just before a run or party. Having church in the morning, kind of like Twisted, Ragman, and I were, meant they were meeting about something of importance. I glanced up at Twisted, and he nodded. He'd caught it too.

"So lay it out here, brother." I liked Mason using that word, because it could mean he was already anticipating meeting our need. "Gimme what you got."

"We've been skirmishing since the last time we talked." That had been during the initial search for the men who had killed my brothers. RWMC had assisted with an intelligence network, the same thing we were hoping to tap into again. "We've gotten some rebuttal from the other group and would formally like to request assistance in tracking down the source of this narrative."

"If you're on a secure line, know that we are too. Lay it out plain, Hitch." Took me a second, but I recognized that voice by its dampened Alabama accent.

"Hoss, thanks, man. Yeah, we've found some lists posted to social media, and we'd like a handle on where they're coming from. Might not mean anything, but it could be something we can use as a direction finder."

"Death lists? Fuck me, man. You and I both know those are a dime a dozen."

"Slate, good to hear you, brother." I'd had several chances to meet the man through the years, and I liked everything about him. "Yeah, but they're very fuckin' specific about who they're targeting, and the idea they'd focus on family is pissin' us right the fuck off."

"Oh, ho. Yeah, that'd earn my displeasure, too." He made a disgusted sound. "Fucking assholes, bringing family into a war."

"This is Myron," a voice interjected, and my insides relaxed just the tiniest amount. If he was already there and ready to go, then we had a chance of getting this underway quickly. "I'll need someone to send me direct links to the lists, and then links to any member's social profiles where family has been targeted. The more information you can feed me up front is work I don't have to do on my own. Saves dozens of steps, and a fuck load of time."

"You got it." Twisted turned to where Ragman was still staring out the window. "Rags, can you have a brother jump on that, man?"

"Yeah." Ragman's response was soft, distracted. "Why haven't we heard back from Sparks yet? If he already had someone rolling, they'd be reporting in by now, surely."

Mason's tense voice came through the speaker. "What's Sparks got to do with anything?"

I remembered too late that the Jailbreakers were an RWMC support club, so by calling Sparks this morning, we'd effectively already involved RWMC in our shit. Deciding direct was the best way to be, I told them the truth. "His sister, Talia, is my old lady. With all this shit goin' down, she stayed back in Florida and I've been calling her regular-like with a burner phone. She missed a check-in with me and now isn't picking up. I called him earlier to have someone get eyes on her to soothe my mind."

"*Shit.*" It sounded as if Gunny, Hoss, and Slate had all spoken at once, with the same tormented word.

"Exactly." My burner picked that moment to ring, and I glanced down to see it was Sparks. "Speak of the devil. Give me a second here." I picked it up, answering in the same moment. "Sparks, we're on the horn with Mason, I'm going to put you on speaker."

"Wait." The soft request stayed my movements, and I clutched the phone tightly. "You need to hear this first. She ain't there, man. She's not there, but we got a note."

I was frozen, unable to respond to him, my mind stunned by his words. Noise rose inside my head. A deafening buzz filled my ears until I couldn't be certain if he'd continued speaking or was waiting for an answer from me. Fingers peeled the phone from my grip, and I heard Ragman say, "Got you on speaker, Sparks. Mason and his crew can hear you, too. What the fuck's going on, man?"

Sparks ripped my heart out with his next words.

"She's been taken. There was a note on her kitchen counter saying as much. She's gone, man. She's fuckin' *gone*." Sparks' voice broke then, and that jerked me from the fugue I'd been descending into. She was his little sister, and I knew in my gut he'd be just as motivated to find her.

Slapping my hands on the tabletop, I barked at the phones, not giving a shit if anyone copped attitude at my tone, "What'd the note say, Sparks? Tell me everything, every-*fucking*-thing. Take a picture of it and text it to me. Have your man go through her place with a fine-toothed comb, see what's out of place, see what's missing if he can.

If they were in her house, that visit wasn't just to leave a note. It was to do something."

Myron cut in, his words firm as they dropped into the conversation. "No. Don't do that. I can have someone there in like twenty minutes. Let my guy go through the house. Have your man step outside. Take the picture of the note but have him put it back where he found it. There's a calling card, I'm sure of it, just like Hitch is, but my guy knows what we're looking for."

The burner dinged where Ragman had laid it back on the table. I reached out and tapped the notification, the screen filling with an image of handwritten words. I read it twice before I allowed the rage to overwhelm me.

"Precious things shouldn't be unattended. Trust me when I say I will give her the attention she deserves. Trust me when I also say she will deeply regret ever knowing you, Hitch."

Twisted's arms wrapped around me from behind, forcing me to drop the chair I'd been battering the walls with. He didn't let go, steadfastly holding me as I screamed at the rafters overhead. He didn't offer false words of comfort, didn't try to tell me that it'd be okay, because like me, he knew that if they had her—and the note was undeniable in its authenticity—if they had her...she was good as dead already.

"No, man. I can't just…" Head back, I stared upwards, fighting the burn in my throat, the stinging behind my eyes. "I can't let her go, brother."

"Nobody's tellin' you to, Hitch. This is me giving you space to get it out of your system." I slowly turned my head, meeting his gaze as he finished, "And this is you pullin' your shit together so we can figure out where we go from here."

"I want her back. No matter what." I couldn't think about what that meant, because in my head, the picture was just Talia before. If I let myself think about what the cartel typically did to collateral, the things they'd been willing to do to leverage their position in the past, I'd fall off the deep end and never surface. "You tell me how we're gonna do that, brother."

"I've got ideas." The voice on the phone caught my attention, and I stared at the device, willing the person to keep talking. "If we move fast and offer to give them what they really want, which is Hitch, then—"

I cut him off quickly. "I'll do it. Whatever's needed."

"Anything to bring her back." Sparks' words overlapped mine.

The man, and I quickly realized it was Myron, started laying out his off-the-cuff plan, and from the brilliance of it, I understood why Mason had kept him close all these years. The man was a genius, straight up.

He finished, and I looked at Twisted, then Ragman, getting nods from both of them. With their blessing, I spoke the words that would pull the trigger on a war-ending campaign. I prayed to God we'd come out the winners.

"Do it."

I Got You

Talia

Shoulders slumped, she feigned unconsciousness, listening closely to her abductors. Their words were in a mix of English and Spanish, with no discernible reason for the flow back and forth between the languages. Her captors had incapacitated her a second time when they first arrived at the current location, and then a third when she'd attempted an ill-conceived escape attempt during a bathroom break. That had led to her current position on the floor, in and out of consciousness, trussed up like a turkey for the oven.

After hours lying on the concrete floor, Talia's shoulders were on fire, pain from the way her arms were bound behind her making itself known. Her hips were in a similar situation, with her lower legs secured together at ankles and knees. Surprisingly, there was no blindfold or gag, and she had watched enough criminal shows to understand that if her captors weren't afraid of her seeing them, it was because they didn't expect her to live long enough to identify them.

"*Amigo*, I'm telling you, this is bad news. Doesn't matter if she's just a booty call for that Incoherent officer, she's a booty call he's gonna be pissed off about when he misses her." From the sound, he was a fair distance away and must have been sitting still, because she couldn't hear him walking.

The other man in the room with her paced back and forth, feet shuffling loudly at every pivot at either end of his path. His voice was higher, more agitated than the first man's. "You think I don't know it's bad news? *Muertos*, when he finds us. The man'll kill us dead. We're nothing, but he won't care we're just soldiers. Man'll kill us dead."

"Why isn't she waking up? Why'd you have to hit her with it again? I think you killed her."

The shuffle sounded sooner than before, and then she heard steps coming her direction. Pins and needles accompanied the nudge against her foot, and she couldn't hold back a groan at the pain. "She ain't dead." Another prodding kick from the man, and she groaned again. "What if she wakes up? We need to know what to do with her. Makes me nervous, man."

Talia opened one eye the barest slit and saw those same cheap black boots topped with threadbare jeans. The man strode away, and she dared a half-lidded glance around the room. Only two men in the large room, but near a large window there were a frightening number of knives and guns on the table where the quiet man sat.

She stared at the knives. In her mind, the blades were sinking into her skin, dragging lines of agony in their wake. It took her a minute to force those ideas away. *Hitch, only Hitch.* Memories flooded her in response, and her next thought was about Hitch. She saw him crouching in front of her, hands covering her cheeks as he lifted her lips to his. *I gotta hold it together. Hitch will come.*

"She's awake."

She'd been so lost in her thoughts that Talia hadn't realized the quiet man had moved closer until pain ripped through her scalp as he lifted her lolling head with a cruel yank on her hair. Without speaking, she narrowed her eyes and glared up at him. In his pock-marked face, his brown eyes were cold as he stared at her. Something flickered across his face, a deep-seated fear she didn't understand.

"You belong to Hitch." He didn't wait for a response, releasing her and standing straight as he turned to his companion. "She gonna get us killed, man. You're right, *amigo*. The scant reward promised isn't worth it." He walked toward the door and paused there, hand on the knob. "*Narco* or no, if you value your life, you'll come with me. You know how this works. We can either go, or we'll go."

"Oh, I know. Hitch kills us if we stay. *Sicario* comes down from the *cerro* and does the job if we leave. We are fucked either way, *amigo*." The steady strides of the other man brought him to stand at Talia's feet. "I say we stay the course."

Maybe I can nudge them.

"Cartel will kill you fast." She pushed her lips up in what she hoped was an aggrieved smile of disinterest. Painfully lifting one shoulder in a shrug, she finished with, "Hitch will take his time. So I guess it's up to you."

Movement in the window made it hard to keep her eyes fixed on the man, but when she realized it was a hovering drone, excitement made her heart race, the accelerating thud in her ears nearly drowning out the man's response. The memory of the screens they'd watched as the club took down the people who had killed Hitch's friends gave her hope.

"You claim Hitch?"

Lifting her chin, Talia told the man directly, "Oh, yeah. He's mine." The presence of the drone seemed like proof positive that she'd been found. *Please, God.* Angling her body forwards, she could have cried from the torment of her shoulders and arms at the new position. Ignoring that as best she could, she threw the rest of her words at the men, praying it would be enough to do whatever distracting her rescuers needed. "If you think to harm him, you'll have to go through his brothers—and mine."

"Who is your brother, *senorita*?" She'd gotten the quiet man's attention.

"Sparks. Jailbreakers MC." Both men flinched and turned to look at each other.

"Did you know?" Quiet man shook his head back and forth. The other one spewed a torrent of Spanish at him, eliciting another headshake.

Hand tightening on the doorknob, the quiet man asked, "How could we not know? They're a Rebel Wayfarers support club, and Rebels are the *capos* in *El Norte*. Now, you and me? We've bought their attention with this. I tell you again, we go, or we'll go. Walking or in a bag."

He took a step back as he opened the door, and that turned into a jarring stumble when the surface rushed in much faster than he'd expected. The doorway filled with men in black leather as the two captors scrambled towards the table where their weapons lay. The large window smashed in an instant later, more bikers entering via that opening. Talia made herself as small as she could, legs drawn up tight to her body. She pressed her head to her knees, hiding her face as a battle raged around her.

A hand lifted her head for the second time in minutes, but this one was infinitely careful. Cradling her chin in his palm, Hitch was crouched in front of her, in almost exactly the position she'd imagined him.

"Tee?" Hitch's voice cracked as he said her name, and Talia let her lids sink closed. "Baby? Look at me." His thumb stroked across her lips. "Beautiful? Hey, beautiful. Are you okay?"

"Hitch?" She finally found her voice and heard his breath catch when she spoke his name. The idea she had that much hold on this man, this beautiful, gorgeous, strong man, humbled her. "I'm okay."

"Look at me, baby." She blinked the wet from her eyes as she opened them, staring at him. Eyes wide, he didn't take his gaze off her, brows drawn together in a deep frown that gave lie to the small smile he tried to keep in place. "There you are. I'm going to get this tape off you." He paused. "You're okay?"

"I'm okay. I'm okay, I promise."

Movement to the side made her glance in that direction, and she found Ewell standing like a statue, gaze fixed on the two of them, a stricken expression on his face. A man she didn't know, one who had a distinctive tattoo on his left arm, stepped up beside Ewell, along with Twisted. They spoke to him, but before he turned to talk to the man with the phoenix tattoo, Ewell mouthed the words, "I love you," to her. Hitch shifted and cut off her view for a few moments, and when he moved out of the way, she could see Ewell had been engulfed within a knot of men, shaking hands with each in what seemed a ritual ended with a back-pounding hug.

It took a couple of minutes, but Hitch released her in fits and starts, seeming unwilling to take his hands off her long enough to cut her free. She watched as he sliced through the tape binding her legs together, peeling it away. Sitting in front of her on the cold floor, he smoothed up and down her legs, thumbs digging into the muscles as she winced and bit her bottom lip. He moved beside her and wrapped his arms around her, easing her to a reclining position the floor. Talia stretched out on her stomach with his assistance, one of his hands holding her head off the grimy floor as he dealt with the bindings on her arms. An instant after he'd freed her, he was ass to the floor and hauling her into his lap as she cried against his shoulder. Hitch stroked her skin everywhere he could reach as he reassured her over and over. "You're okay. I'm here. I got you."

Ch-ch-ch-Changes

Hitch

She cried in my arms, the pain of blood and feeling returning to her limbs washing over her in waves, and I held her through it all. Sparks came over at one point and took a knee next to us, one trembling hand lifted to smooth down Talia's hair. I met his eyes over her head and accepted every ounce of recrimination I saw there.

Thirty-six hours.

She'd been in hell for a day and a half because of her association with me.

That knowledge hurt like hell, but even as I silently acknowledged it to him, I knew it didn't matter one whit. She was mine, and I was keeping her.

I'd already told Twisted my plans for after we recovered her. There'd been no doubt in my mind that we would be successful, and I'd refused to allow myself to consider her being in anything other than whole and healthy form when we did.

Even as we were busting through the door, I'd been drawn to where she'd been huddled against the wall like she was my true north.

I hadn't paid a lick of attention to the fight surging quick and deadly around me. Screams and gurgles, the sound of fists against faces, or the finality of a knife to a throat— nothing mattered except Talia. I'd bulled through arrow-straight to her side, and it had been the work of moments to free her. Now it was two hours later and I was still on my ass with Talia in my lap. There'd been a full dozen of Sparks' men come to pay respects, and I knew why.

They expected to lose her to me.

Little did the fuckers know they'd be gaining one large pain in their collective asses.

"Baby?" I gave it a minute, but when she didn't respond, I jostled her gently and tried again. "Baby doll, wake up, honey. You with me, Tee?"

"Mmhmm?" My woman sounded about half asleep, and I empathized, but we needed to vacate the premises fairly soon, so I couldn't indulge myself beyond what I'd already done.

"We gotta get in the wind, baby." I shoved an arm under her legs and levered myself against the wall to stand, carefully holding her against my chest. "You're gonna ride with me."

"On the bike?" She stirred in my arms, head lifting so I could see her face. The bruising would fade within days, as would the burns from the Taser they'd used to incapacitate her. I'd expected to see fear or at least a hesitancy in her eyes, waiting long moments until I could believe maybe they wouldn't appear. "We never got to do that before."

"Yeah, baby. On the bike. You and me are gonna head to your place." She gave me a surprised frown, and that made me grin. "I wanna see your crib, baby. Wanna pick apart your decorating style, make a place for me there."

"My place?" She twisted slightly and I released her legs, letting her slide slowly down with our fronts pressed together. The softly giving flesh traveling down my length had my cock waking up and taking notice. *Down boy*, I told myself. *Not until we're alone.*

"Yeah, darlin'. Now, can you ride, or you need another minute to wake up?"

"I can ride." Her chin lifted, and I swooped down to take her mouth in response to her clear demand. The gentle caresses of my lips on hers weren't enough, but I forced myself to pull back.

"Let's roll."

Twisted stalked across the room before Talia and I could walk outside, an expression on his face I didn't understand until I saw what was in his hands: a curve of a top rocker and bulky fabric of a brand-new center patch. Instead of the expected nameless face behind bars the Jailbreakers sported, it was a skull holding a key tight in its mouth.

Seemed I wouldn't be joining the Jailbreakers MC after all.

My gaze lifted to where Mason stood next to Ragman. The two men were in an intense conversation, but as if he felt the weight of my stare on him, Mason found my eyes across the room. He nodded slowly, then gave me the slightest of chin lifts.

Son of a bitch.

~ ~ Fini ~ ~

THANK YOU SO MUCH FOR READING
No Man's Land!

I truly hope you enjoyed this crossover story tying things together even tighter between the Rebel Wayfarers MC and the Neither This Nor That MC sagas. Thanks for takin' this trip along with me.

~ML

ABOUT THE AUTHOR

Raised in the south, *Wall Street Journal* & *USA TODAY* bestselling author MariaLisa learned about the magic of books at an early age. Every summer, she would spend hours in the local library, devouring books of every genre. Self-described as a book-a-holic, she says "I've always loved to read, but then I discovered writing, and found I adored that, too. For reading...if nothing else is available, I've been known to read the back of the cereal box."

Want sneak peeks into what she's working on, or to chat with other readers about her books? Join the Facebook group! **bit.ly/deMora-FB-group**

deMora's got a spam-free newsletter list she'd love to have you join, too: **bit.ly/mldemora-newsletter**

~~~~~
~~~~~

My Rebel Wayfarers MC and the Neither This Nor That MC series do cross over, along with the Occupy Yourself band books, so readers have a couple of choices. The series can be read independently beginning with RWMC, OYBS, and then NTNT without too many spoilers. There's also a crossover between my RWMC world and Lila Rose's Hawks MC world. Or they can be read intertwined—in chronological order.

Here's the recommended reading order if you want to follow according to timing:

Mica, RWMC #1

A Sweet & Merry Christmas, RWMC #1.5

Slate, RWMC #2

Bear, RWMC #3

Born Into Trouble, OYBS #1

Jase, RWMC #4

Gunny, RWMC #5

Mason, RWMC #6

Hoss, RWMC #7

This Is the Route of Twisted Pain, NTNT #1

Harddrive Holidays, RWMC #7.5

Duck, RWMC #8

Biker Chick Campout, RWMC #8.5

Watcher, RWMC #9

Treading the Traitor's Path: Out Bad, NTNT #2

Living Without, Lila Rose's Hawks MC: Caroline Springs #4

Shelter My Heart, NTNT #3

A Kiss to Keep You, RWMC #9.25

Gun Totin' Annie, RWMC #9.5

Secret Santa, RWMC #9.75

Trapped by Fate on Reckless Roads, NTNT #4

Bones, RWMC #10

Gunny's Pups, RWMC #10.25

Not Even A Mouse, RWMC #10.75

Road Runner's Ride, RWMC #12.5

Never Settle, RWMC #10.5

Fury, RWMC #11

Christmas Doings, RWMC #11.25

Gypsy's Lady, RWMC #11.5

Thunderstruck, NTNT #5

Going Down Easy

No Man's Land

Cassie, RWMC #12

~~~~~

Also by MariaLisa deMora

Neither This Nor That MC romance series

Legends are born from moments like these. Folktales spun around a single point in time so perfect, you can almost hear the click resonating through the universe as things align. Meet Twisted, Po'Boy, Retro,
~~~~~

and Ragman, good old boys from southern states who have many things in common. First, is a bone-deep love of the biker lifestyle. Second, would be their love of the brotherhood, and knowing that you trust the man at your back. Finally, these men have the love of a good woman. None of these come without a price, and it is our pleasure to journey along with them as they discover the blessings that can be won, and lost along the way.

> *This is the Route of Twisted Pain*
> *Treading the Traitor's Path: Out Bad*
> *Shelter My Heart*
> *Trapped by Fate on Reckless Roads*
> *Thunderstruck*

5-Star Reviews for the stories of the NTNT MC series

This is the Route of Twisted Pain
"This is the Route of Twisted Pain is an exhilarating, gripping romance novel contrived of incredible world building, complex yet relatable characters, and a unique, captivating plot.
Gifted storyteller MariaLisa deMora beautifully balances exciting suspense, fast action, intriguing secrets with delicious, blazing hot romance scenes. Readers will be up all night with this riveting page-turner."
~ NY Literary Magazine

I am completely tickled in my fancy for TWISTED!
First off, let me state that there was one thing I didn't
like about this book and that is the LAST PAGE! I hated
for it to end. I dearly loved this book and its characters
as well as their setting.
~Colleen M.

Gripping tale
Twisted and Penny fit together beautifully. The book
covers so much more than just their love story. Great
introduction to the Incoherent MC. The tale is gripping
and gritty. The journey is full of twists and turns that
keep you on the edge of your seat. I couldn't put it
down. Cannot wait for the next one.
~Lillmil

Twisted is one of the most original and interesting
characters I have read in a long time. Marialisa's
character building is setting a high bar for her to
follow, she will hopefully continue with Po'Boy's story.
The Route of Twisted Pain was pure brilliance, and I
highly recommend this read.
~Penny T.

This book obsessed me!
This may be the best book I read all year.
These people...they're not characters, they're real...
have stuck in my head from the day I met them.
MariaLisa deMora can throw words down that'll Twist
(hehe) your insides up till you can't breathe for
waiting to hear what's next!
I'm working my way through her other 'families' and
yup....she really is that good.
~DeLane

Treading the Traitor's Path: Out Bad
"Treading the Traitor's Path: Out Bad is a solidly engrossing, well-written novel by a talented author. MariaLisa deMora delivers a thrilling ride filled with exciting suspense, deliciously explicit, vivid sex scenes, and gritty, fast-paced action. Her characters are smart, complex, and strong with sharp edges. The settings meticulously detailed.
Fans of Motorcycle Club romance stories will not want to miss this second installment in deMora's exciting series."
~ NY Literary Magazine
What an amazing read! DeMora does not simply wrote a book, she pulls you into a different world. When you read her work, you are very much surrounded by the characters and setting. Prepare for a book hangover because once you finish the book, you will still be stuck with Po Boy.
~KW

THIS WAS AMAZING. Highly recommend for a good story line, interesting characters. I just wish there was more more more.
~Laura

Loved This Book!
What did I just read?! Is my kindle still working? I'm pretty sure it combusted into flames while reading this story. RED HOT READ for 2017. Not what I was expecting at all! I tend to stay away from ménage a trois, because for me it's hard to say there's any kind of conflict except for jealousy, and the ending kind of

leaves things unresolved and unrealistic. NOT THIS BOOK! The best one out there guaranteed.
~Linda A

...seriously this series is just WTF so freaking good. Dark, Twisted, harsh, painful and raw. Po'Boy lives for his club, his brothers and his family, there is nothing he wouldn't do for them.
~Fay

I live and breathe for books like this! Fabulously Naughty!...Wickedly Hot! This is my first book by MariaLisa deMora and it will not be my last. MariaLisa delivered a 5 STAR READ! The plot is filled with action, suspense, romance and tons of hot scenes.
~Jenny F

~~~~~

Alace Sweets, a dark romantic suspense standalone

A dark thriller, this book is not a light read. Filled with edge-of-your-seat suspense, this intense story commands the reader's attention as it drives towards the explosive ending. Alace Sweets is a vigilante serial killer, with everything that implies and is sure to trip all your triggers. Be ready.
~~~~~

At seventeen, Alace Sweets turned a corner in her life, taking the wrong shortcut home from school.

Resisting the harsh knowledge her attackers will never be made to pay for their actions, Alace takes a stand. Justice must be served, and if fate's scales are out of balance, she's determined to set things right as best she can.

When the laws of men fail, the rules of Alace prevail.

5-Star Reviews for Alace Sweets

"Whatever deep dark trench [deMora] pulled a character like Alace from should be revisited again and often."
~Confessions of a Serial Reader

"deMora has a superb story-line and exceptional character development. All of her characters have such depth that will intrigue the reader..."
~Turning Another Page

"Hot, sweet, dark thriller."
~Beth D

"It will keep you on the edge of your seat and give you chills."
~Escape Reality Book Blog

"Disturbing, haunting, sickly; yet hot, sexy and heart racing!"
~Amanda L

"From the first page [deMora] pulls you into the world she has created and you do not even try to escape..."
~Little Shop of Readers Blog

"A must read for all those dark, gritty romance fans out there."
~Sweet & Spicy Reads

"You will find yourself so drawn into the story that the outside world is blocked out and your locking the doors and turning on all the lights."
~Danena F

"Don't judge me for bonding with a vigilante serial killer, she's more than what she does."
~iScream Books

"Thrilling...chilling...full of suspense, nail biting edge of your seat excitement."
~Tracey H

"Every time MariaLisa deMora picks up her pen (or opens her computer), she creates characters you want to believe in."
~Gail S

"Intriguing dark storyline, beautiful love story and nail-biting conclusion, what more could a reader ask for?"

~Manda M

"This book takes you a dark and twisted ride that is gripping…"
~Renee Entress' Blog

"This book is dark and gritty and I literally had to take a day off from reading it because it's that intense."
~My Girlfriend's Couch

"This is my favourite book so far from this author … I recommend this book if you enjoy dark romantic thrillers."
~Cheekypee Reads and Reviews

"There's not enough stars to give this book and 5 just doesn't really do it justice!"
~DeLane C

"I couldn't put this book down from page one! Tried to stop & go to bed but couldn't sleep thinking about Alace and got up & finished the book."
~Debbie M

"MariaLisa DeMora, wordsmith that she is, made this a story of the enlightenment of a woman and finding love in a life where she has had none."
~Kat W

~~~~~

Hard Focus, a criminal thriller standalone

This is an intense page-turner, a gut-punch twist-filled story about a woman who has confidence in herself, believes she's a good judge of character, and has filled her life with people she can trust. She's right, but she's also very, very wrong. Readers will have a time of it trying to decide who to watch closest.

Where do you place your trust when your own instincts betray you?

Connie Rowe is a receptionist at a respected legal firm. She's a little bit sassy, a lotta bit happy, has good friends, and is adored by her neighbors.

Life is good.

She's got a boyfriend she enjoys spending time with. He can be a little intense, but he's got a lot going on in his own life, sorting out his young daughter and nightmare of an ex.

Life is grand.
~~~~~

"Trust your gut." That's what Connie's police officer father told her often, training his daughter to believe in herself through the years.

But ... what happens when you can't? When your intuition lies?

What happens when things come into Hard Focus?

5-Star Reviews for Hard Focus

"Hard Focus is one very well-written tale. 5 stars is not enough for me."
~Tabitha

"What a powerful story. [deMora] kept me invested from the first word to the last."
~Jesse R

"[deMora] has a certain magical touch to writing her characters, that they become either your nemesis, your best friend, or your love interest. That is certainly portrayed in this spin around. Loved it, loved it, loved it."
~Sandy K

"I strongly recommend this book for both entertainment and to broaden your knowledge of certain laws that must be revisited."
~Words Turn Me On

"A intense page turner. Once you start, you can't put the book down."
~Tracey H

"A beautifully written, powerful read that I can't rate highly enough. This story will stay with me always."
~Gayle

"This book had twists I didn't see coming. Loved it!"

~Lori R

"Wow! I am in awe of deMora's skill in crafting this story."
~Kat W

"I keep sayin that there just aren't enough stars to give to some of Marialisa deMora's books...this one is no different!"
~deLane

"Where do I start with this one...I read this in 3 1/2 hours uninterrupted, I absolutely could NOT put it down. Very deep, keeps you guessing, what's gonna happen next, kind of book. I love how strong her characters are, especially the females!"
~Wendy I

"Sometimes I feel like MariaLisa deMora is the one I should be watching out for. I started reading her books because I'm addicted to MC Romance, but then she decides to change things up and I just follow her wherever she leads me like a Pied Piper. I never know

what to expect, and sometimes I'm afraid to find out, but it's always an adventure."
~Rosa for iScream Books Blog

"A plot full of twists and turns, a story that's not quite what it seems, strong characterization, jaw dropping revelations... what more do you need from a book?"
~Manda M

"This book kept me turning the pages wondering what was going to happen. I am usually pretty good at guessing twists but not with this book. She totally surprised me and brought me out of my funk. 5 stars."
~Glenna M

"What an amazing story! Filled with a smidge of suspense, a dash of action and a heap of realism of our country's laws and how their vague application to victims can adversely affect its citizens and the people in their lives."
~Naughty Mom Story Time

ADDITIONAL SERIES AND BOOKS

Please note that books in a series frequently feature characters from additional books within that series. If series books are read out of order, readers will twig to spoilers for the other books, so going back to read the skipped titles won't have the same angsty reveals.

Rebel Wayfarers MC series:

Mica, #1
A Sweet & Merry Christmas, #1.5
Slate, #2
Bear, #3
Jase, #4
Gunny, #5
Mason, #6
Hoss, #7
Harddrive Holidays, #7.5
Duck, #8
Biker Chick Campout, #8.5
Watcher, #9
A Kiss to Keep You, #9.25
Gun Totin' Annie, #9.5
Secret Santa, #9.75
Bones, #10
Gunny's Pups, #10.25
Never Settle, #10.5
Not Even A Mouse, #10.75
Fury, #11
Christmas Doings, #11.25
Gypsy's Lady, #11.5
Cassie, #12
Road Runner's Ride, #12.5

Occupy Yourself band series:

Born Into Trouble, #1
Grace In Motion, #2 (TBD)
What They Say, #3 (TBD)

Neither This, Nor That MC series:

This Is the Route Of Twisted Pain, #1
Treading the Traitor's Path: Out Bad, #2
Shelter My Heart, #3
Trapped by Fate on Reckless Roads, #4
Thunderstruck, #5

Rebel Wayfarers & Incoherent MC (NTNT) crossover stories:

Going Down Easy
No Man's Land

Mayhan Bucklers MC series:

Most Rikki-Tik, #1
Mad Minute, #2
Pucker Factor, #3
Boocoo Dinky Dau, #4

Borderline Freaks MC series:

Service and Sacrifice, #1
More Than Enough, #2
Lack of Inbetween, #3
See You in Valhalla, #4

If You Could Change One Thing:
Tangled Fates Stories

There Are Limits, #1
Rules Are Rules, #2
The Gray Zone, #3

Other Books:

With My Whole Heart
Alace Sweets
Hard Focus
Dirty Bitches MC: Season 3

More information available at **mldemora.com**.